FOLLOW ME

FOLLOW ME

—·—·—·—·—·—·—·—

PAUL GRINER

—·—·—·—·—·—·—·—

RANDOM HOUSE

NEW YORK

The following stories have been previously published: "Clouds" appeared in *Bomb*;
"Thief" appeared in *Caesura*; "Nails" appeared in *Glimmer Train*; "Worboys'
Transaction" appeared in *The Graywolf Annual Four*; "Boxes" appeared in *Playboy*;
"Grass" appeared in *Ploughshares*; and "Follow Me" and "Back Home Again" appeared
in *Story*.

The author extends special thanks to Sophie Calle for her permission to mingle fact
and fiction.

Library of Congress Cataloging-in-Publication Data
Griner, Paul.
Follow me / Paul Griner.—1st ed.
p.   cm.
ISBN 0-679-44845-4
I. Title.
PS3557.R5314F65   1996
813'.54—dc20   95-43102

Printed in the United States of America on acid-free paper
24689753
First Edition

For Anne

Acknowledgments

Thanks are especially due to Chris Kennedy, Lynne McFall, and Toby Wolff for their repeated, thoughtful readings of these stories. I would also like to thank my editor, Dan Menaker, for his insightful comments and strong support; his assistant, Adam Davies; and the rest of the people at Random House who made this collection possible. And I would like to thank Nicole Aragi— a wonderful agent whom any writer would be lucky to have; Gloria Loomis, who first took me on; and Lily Oei, all at Watkins/Loomis. And finally, the greatest thanks of all to my wife, Anne, who believed when no one else even knew.

Contents

FOLLOW ME

FOLLOW ME

—·—·—·—·—·—·—·—·—

"**F**ollow me," she said to John Spadafore. He was a private investigator. His ad said he was the best photo man in the business. *"So good they don't even know I'm there."* That would fit her project perfectly. She was sitting in his office.

"What?" Spadafore said, leaning forward in his chair. "You want me to follow you?" He was a small man, so short his feet didn't touch the ground. The back of his chair loomed above him like a throne. His tight blond curls looked sewn onto his head; his blue suit glowed.

She could see the pictures in her mind's eye, glossy, grainy. She would dress up for different roles. A flared short skirt, black high heels, a flash of white thigh when she twirled. No panties under this one. Or: looking ragged the morning after a late party—smeared lipstick, a chiffon scarf to hide her ratty hair, dark glasses despite the gray sky (no shadows in the background), a cigarette stuck in her mouth, her hand out toward the camera as if to block it. Or: her surprised face at the door when she answers a stranger's ring, clutching her terry robe to her throat, the lock chain stretching from cheek to cheek. In the right light the picture would lack all depth; the chain would look flat across her face, like a tattoo.

She struck a match and lit her cigarette, then shook the match out slowly, aware that he was watching her long, slim fingers. She buttoned the high collar of her sweater, unbuttoned it, buttoned it again, and blew smoke toward the ceiling. "Yes. I want you to follow me and take my picture. That shouldn't be hard, should it?" As she sat forward she could feel her sweater tightening across her chest. She glanced around the cluttered office and mentally rearranged some of the furniture. This is how it should be: dusty papers sliding off opened books, a chair too nicely centered beneath a window, a lamp shade throwing its long shadow on a wall. If she were photographing it she would want it to look effortless, seamless, to look like real life and yet be just a little more profound. Then she decided the room would be better as it was, like some magical found object.

"God, it really is like a bad book, isn't it?" she said.

"What is?" The blond curls retreated from Spadafore's forehead as he raised his eyebrows.

She smiled. "Never mind." She stood and extracted a fat coffee-colored envelope from her purse. "Here's two hundred and fifty dollars." It was all in singles, so the envelope would look thicker. She wished she could get a shot of herself handing the envelope over, but he was not to know that she was a photographer or the whole concept would be ruined. Perhaps he had a camera hidden somewhere, shooting away, just in case. What would he do if she pulled out a gun? She dropped the envelope on his desk and watched papers flutter off both sides like butterflies. On the tripod, at a fast shutter speed, with Spadafore's brogans visible beneath the desk, the Leica would turn that into a stunning series.

"Just follow me for a day, take some pictures. Leave them in my mailbox in the same envelope. You can keep the negatives." She snapped the purse shut and twisted the bracelet circling her wrist. His gaze lingered where her fingers had touched her white skin. "If I like your work, I'll hire you for a couple of weeks. I wrote my address on one of the bills."

She left before he could say anything else.

Ten days later the pictures were in her mailbox. Bright colors, standard white borders. Some she was prepared for. She'd seen him lurking in a doorway across from her apartment, spotted his truck following her as she strolled up Greene Street to her gallery. Several good shots she hadn't known were coming—they were taken at odd angles, as if he had been lying on the ground while she walked away, or were slightly off-center, her back and profile against a chainlink fence—not just the standard head shots. She sent the pictures back, each of them ripped in half. Across one she scrawled, "Black and white are the colors of photography. Color film is worthless." It irritated her that she hadn't thought to tell him that at first. She included five hundred dollars this time.

She posed in front of the Marden Gallery—when she saw Spadafore's truck—looking bored, angry, amused. Her first

show had been there, two years before. She wondered if anyone would get the reference.

The Marden show had been an unexpected success. She
had been playing with forms then, wondering why photography exhibits were always a gray band at eye level, when a
friend of a friend offered her some space. It wasn't a gallery,
really—more of a hallway someone had to pass through, a
kind of lobby, on the way to a hair salon. The acrid smell of
permanent solution filled the air, the light was poor, and
without looking up no one would even notice the installa-
tion. She loved it anyway; it was the first place she'd ever
been given.

She displayed six photographs, all of them life-size: one
of a three-foot square of the ceiling, one of each of the hallway's four corners, and one of the juncture between two
walls and the ceiling. The corner pictures were hung in the
corners, the ceiling picture on the ceiling, and the picture
of the two walls and the ceiling was mounted at the juncture
of the walls and the floor, a mirror image. All of them save
one were framed and double matted, to give them some remove, and she made the frames herself. Each took a day to
complete, except the corner and ceiling picture frame, which
was more ambitious. She spent two weeks getting that one
perfect. The ceiling picture frame was simple, and, when she
came to the last corner photograph, out of money, she left
it unmatted and unframed. After hanging it, she decided the
picture was better that way, more disorienting. The photograph overlaid the wall exactly so that each became an ex-
tension of the other. A crack meandering across the picture
wandered onto the plaster, ending a foot above the floor.

Luckily, one of the hair salon's clients was a critic for the *Times,* which published a small, respectful review, two paragraphs in the middle of the arts page in the Weekend section. It appeared on the next-to-the-last day of the show. The reviewer noted the peculiar framing and location of the pictures, and argued that they exemplified the artist's meaning: that the simplest things can sometimes be menacing. She concluded by saying, "The pictures took on an importance far beyond and above their representational value, as if they were something lurking in the corners, like bats. Corners will no longer be corners, to this reviewer, and that's quite an accomplishment."

The next gallery she wanted to show at was DeKLERK! on Greene Street, in SoHo. She had already surveyed it, dressed as a gawking tourist, noting the receptionist's clothes, the wall colors, the gallery's style. They'd had African drum music turned up too loud that day. Wearing her leathers and a bright handmade Egyptian pin, and armed with the review, she talked DeKlerk himself into holding her next show. He complimented her imitation-leopard-skin ankle band and said he hoped her show would be as interesting.

This time she wanted people as subjects. On hot June mornings she walked up Wall Street and Fifth Avenue, slipping her card into the windows of expensive cars that were cracked open a bit against the heat, sometimes pressing her lips to the card and leaving behind a blot of lipstick, other times spraying it with her perfume. The entire car would smell of her when the drivers returned.

She used different-colored lipsticks to see which inspired

more calls, then sat at home icing her sore feet, spending
weeks listening to the messages. When men called—it was
safe enough, an answering service, an imaginary name—she
called back hoping to arrange a meeting at the bandstand in
Carl Schurz Park. On the phone they were blunt, aggressive,
timid, scared; three quarters told her she was crazy and hung
up. Several asked if she was a hooker; they sounded the most
interested, and the more perverse they became the more certain she was they would show. She didn't care. She knew
she'd never meet them. She told them all to wear a raincoat
with a red rose in the lapel and to carry a white umbrella.
That way, she said, she'd recognize them. She photographed
them from across the park when they arrived and planned
to call the series "Meetings." Twenty-five men out of the
hundreds she'd called, all dressed the same, all captured
against the same bandstand. They must have been mad. In
the first prints the roses came out dark; she painted them
over to make them black.

Three women phoned, two asking for a date. Another
said, "Listen, bitch. This is Bobi Edmonds. I know you've
been here; I've smelled your perfume. Leave my husband
alone." Pissed off one day, unhappy with the project's
progress, she looked up Bobi Edmonds' address in the Manhattan phone book, then took photos of her own legs while
sitting on a Louis XVI chair. She wore nothing garish, white
lace stockings and black satin pumps. The photos showed her
thighs and the chair and the stockings and the shoes and, at
the top edge, the beginnings of garters. She sent six prints,
each print eleven by fourteen inches and taken from a slightly
different angle, the difference so slight one would have to

study them to find it. She was certain Mrs. Edmonds would. In lipstick, on the back of one, she wrote, "He wanted these."

To make up and send the package took time from her work, but she was glad she'd done it; it gave her the idea for another series, called "Legs." She knew it would be a good one. Tumbling along on the river of its possibilities she sketched it out in her mind—the shots, the victims, the look. She paced her apartment, jotting notes on napkins, old magazines, the back of bills. She always had this kind of reaction when an idea was good. She imagined the critical reception, the toadying of a few gallery owners trying to woo her away from DeKLERK!, glossy coffee-table books with her name written in thirty-six-point type across the bottom.

It would be a series of pictures of her stockinged legs, indoors and out, in her studio, sitting on a curb, riding city buses. She didn't want to do it in New York; New Yorkers wouldn't care what she did on the street or while riding buses and she wanted a reaction. She'd have to leave the city to get it. She threw an overnight bag and some equipment into her car and drove upstate until she came to Auburn, a small city where the light seemed permanently smoky. Stepping out onto a cobbled side street she knew she'd come to the right place—the unhurried pace of the five o'clock traffic, the crumbling brick facades on the downtown buildings, the storefront churches and lottery shops. JESUS SAVES, she saw over and over. Street after street smelled of diesel exhaust.

When she boarded a bus she took off her raincoat and sat down, aiming the camera at her legs. Her skirt was mid-thigh. She wore the same lace stockings she'd photographed herself in before. She took roll after roll, her ears growing accustomed to the engine's rumble. Soon, above it, she heard people whisper, the rustle of their clothes as they turned or pointed. Ten minutes into each ride she lifted the camera and began photographing the other passengers, most of them in the act of turning away, frowning their disapproval.

The bus passed an old stone prison with medieval-looking turrets and crenellations. She got out, spread her raincoat on the curb opposite the high prison wall, sat on it. She photographed herself again. When she looked up, a guard was peering down at her from a stone tower, above the wall. She took his picture, walked across the street, took more of him. He leaned out so far, she thought he was going to fall onto the razor wire on top of the wall. With the last of her film she recorded the street, making sure both the place she sat and the prison were in the frame.

At the gallery she hung all the photographs on hinged frames, alternating shots of her legs with portraits: the raincoated men who had come to meet her in the park, the bus riders, the prison guard. Pulling open the portrait frames revealed another photograph mounted on the wall, her with her camera, looking at the viewer, as if about to take his or her photo. Behind the photographs of her legs were mirrors—the viewer suddenly become voyeur.

The men fell into sections entitled "Perfume" or "Lipstick." The accompanying notes explained how she'd come to take their photographs. The shots of her legs were in progression. The first twenty or so looked identical, though

they weren't—legs, shoes, stockings, thighs, chair. In the
next one a man's hand appeared on her knee, then came
more without any seeming variation. Across the front of
one she lipsticked, "He wanted these." In the last leg shot—
and the last photograph of the show—a blur moved across
the bottom of the frame and one of the garter's was un-
snapped, the stocking beginning to sag.

She stood in a gallery corner and watched viewers take
note of the hinges, hesitate, reach forward to open them.
Some never did, afraid to break the taboo against touching
art. She photographed those she guessed were critics, all of
them from behind and in unflattering light. It hadn't come
to her yet how but she knew she would use these in another
show. One critic dismissed the hinged frames—and the
show—as a gimmick. All the critics picked up on the
anonymity of the men in the portraits, their interchange-
ability. The best review was by Holly Carter, who had seen
her work at the salon. She devoted a whole page to it in the
Times and included two pictures.

"Some of the photographs are the size of doors," Carter
wrote. "Others operate more as windows. The pictures almost stand for entrances and exits, allowing the viewer to
enter and disappear within.

"The 'Legs' series, by the way, is astonishingly powerful.
Where her legs come together is shadowed, the darkness
hinting at promise. In the last of the series, with its un-
snapped garter, one doesn't know whether the blurred hand
at the bottom is moving toward or away. I've never seen anything so erotic."

The review's last line ran continually before her eyes like

the electronic message board in Times Square. "What she can do from here is nearly unimaginable."

She put an ad in the personals. She would date the men, a few times. They were happy to meet someone so pretty on a blind date. If they were married and she liked them she fucked them. Leaning over them, her legs straddling their chests, she whispered that she wanted to take their photograph. Most balked, worried the pictures might get out. She climbed off, swore they wouldn't, dabbed perfume inside her elbows while they watched. If they agreed she climbed back on. If they didn't she told them to leave. With her fingertips, she closed the eyelids of all who stayed. "Just for one shot," she said. Though the men submitted, their eyelids trembled beneath her touch like the wings of captured birds. Still, they didn't protest. The hard part had been getting them to let her shoot at all. After that, she realized, nearly anything was possible.

At some point she told each of the men—whether she'd slept with them or not—that she had a surprise for him. She asked them to meet her on the same street corner around 8:00 P.M. Most stood under an arc lamp, in the center of its funnel of light, afraid, perhaps, that they might get jumped. The lamp rose directly in front of her gallery and she positioned herself inside, in the darkness, watching them. None of the men ever noticed her picture in the window and none thought to search for her behind it.

By the time she was ten minutes late they began to pace. Some smiled, some seemed angry, some appeared worried. At one time or another they all jammed their hands into their

pockets. The moment they started to walk off, looking fool-
ish, she photographed them.

This series she called "Leavings." Many came out slightly
blurred, which she liked; it gave them the look of movement.
The fuck pictures were still, the faces explicitly clear in a
harsh light, as if they had been taken at a morgue. Only her
knees pressed against the men's chests and the rumpled
sheets visible at the pictures' margins revealed that they
weren't. She titled this series "Dead."

In the press release she said she'd fucked only married
men, and noted that the pictures were taken in the act. "Pro-
fessionals, every one of them," she said. Two or three threatened to sue when they heard about the show. She told them
they shouldn't have been doing it. They never called again,
perhaps afraid of what she might do next.

She hung the "Leavings" pictures waist-high around the
gallery. Viewers would have to bend over to see them
clearly, and when they did, they would notice footprints
painted on the floor with letters indicating where the viewers should stand. In between the footprints was a frame. If
she hadn't fucked someone, she left the floor frame empty;
if she had, she filled it with his "Dead" shot. Standing over
the photographs, the viewers were in the same position she
had been in when she'd photographed the naked men.

When the exhibit opened, the line outside the gallery
stretched a block and a half, mostly women. She wondered
how many of them were wives looking for their husbands'
faces in order to buy those pictures before anyone else saw
them.

The exhibit catapulted her to fame. Though not a single

review noted where she'd taken the photographs, nearly all claimed she had established herself as a major talent with this show. Pace Gallery sent an admiring note and suggested she stop by with her portfolio. *ARTnews* and *Artforum* did spreads. For the latter, she insisted on taking her own portrait. Secretly, she worried they'd turn down the whole project. Black-and-white, of course, half her face in a mirror. The other half, and half the camera, cropped by the mirror frame. The hidden camera, it seemed to be saying. Who's watching who? They used it on the cover.

The notoriety thrilled her, spurred her to try something even more daring. Why not make herself her own subject? The legs were only the start. She was convinced the critics would like it even more than her last show. She knew it would be her best group. She would call it "Me."

She set up cameras in her apartment and in her studio with automatic timers, so that they would go off at unexpected times, but something was missing; she knew where the cameras were and, roughly, when they would snap. There was no surprise, no mystery, no sense of danger. That was when she got the idea of going to a private investigator and asking him to photograph her. She pored over every ad in the Yellow Pages before choosing Spadafore. His was so goofy that he had to be the right one. True, she'd know he was following her, but not always where or when. The thought thrilled her, made her quiver.

She was inundated with photographs. The day she posed in front of the Marden Gallery she also posed in front of DeKLERK!, standing beneath the same lamp her subjects had. She kept her hands in her pockets. Spadafore photographed her from a different angle, but she knew a sharp observer would notice the same graffiti scrawled on the brick wall behind her that appeared in a corner of the "Leavings" pictures. "One must wonder," she imagined the critics writing, "if this is some kind of hint—of her 'Exit' from the scene, or from this kind of photography, or this medium?"

After a month she sent Spadafore a check for a thousand dollars. More photographs came, envelope after envelope. Seemingly as a joke, the envelopes were always the same coffee color she'd first given him. She had more shots than she needed for a show. She sent him another check, this one for five hundred dollars, and wrote that she had enough photos and thanked him for his services. He hadn't cashed the first check. More envelopes came, one a day for a week. At first she was amused. She thought Spadafore had developed a crush on her and went to see him. A typing service now occupied his former office. Spadafore's name still arced across the pebbled glass window, and when she pointed this out to the typists their manager said the door was being changed within the week. She went downstairs and around the corner to a phone booth and looked up Spadafore's number in the Yellow Pages. When she dialed it, a recorded message told her that the number had been disconnected and that no new number was in service. When she got home, there was another envelope full of pictures and the letter she'd sent to him with the first five-hundred-dollar check inside. Stamped in purple ink across the envelope were the words ADDRESSEE UNKNOWN.

She went to the public library and searched through the five boroughs' phone books for his name or a home phone number. Finding nothing, she enlarged her search: New Jersey, Long Island, up the Hudson. The pictures kept coming. Scared, she went to the police. The station smelled of smoke and sweat; three men were shackled to a bench.

The police told her they couldn't do anything unless Spadafore actually threatened her.

"The pictures are threatening," she said, laying some on the sergeant's desk.

The sergeant leafed through them. "They seem like nice enough pictures to me. They're all taken on the street, nothing invasive about that." He studied two, tugging on his ear. "You look good in pictures, you know that?"

"I don't want them taken. Isn't that threatening enough?"

The sergeant drank some coffee and shook his head. "What you want isn't really the issue here. As long as it's outside, he can take pictures of anyone he feels like." He finished the coffee, turned the Styrofoam cup upside down on his desk, and crumpled it with the heel of his palm. It made a slight popping noise. "Even you," he said, handing the pictures back to her, wiping a drop of coffee from the top one with his thumb.

Suddenly, the pictures stopped coming. She had lost a great deal of time trying to track down Spadafore, and her show was scheduled to start in two weeks. She threw herself into the work of sorting, choosing, arranging. She photographed the best of Spadafore's photographs, enlarging some, shrinking others. She papered one exhibition wall with a giant print of herself taken in front of the gallery, standing beneath the lamp, and used it as background for the other photos.

Again, the show was a success. DeKlerk, dressed in his trademark black, his shaved head glistening, pulled her aside to tell her that someone from the Whitney had set up an appointment to discuss a one-woman show. She stayed out partying for two days. Home finally, she slept for sixteen hours and awoke to the buzzing of her doorbell. Federal Express. Pictures.

A series of them from the opening of "Me." Her in front of pictures of herself, signing someone's program, sandwiched among three people. The person's program she was signing had his or her back to the camera and was leaning toward her; she couldn't tell if it was a man or a woman. The one of her with the three people had been doctored. The people had been whited out, like angels, or something more menacing. She didn't remember Spadafore at the reception, though there had been a crowd and he certainly could have gotten lost. But he would have stood out in his shiny suit, and without an invitation he shouldn't have been able to get through the door.

Another package came the next day, and the next. She looked in the new phone book, and now even Spadafore's ad was gone. All the letters she wrote came back. Packages kept arriving. She became distracted; her work suffered. She went to her mailbox daily, occasionally finding the fat envelopes, bulging with pictures and always the same coffee color; they all had New York postmarks. If she found one she opened a bottle of red wine and drank it while looking through the photographs, then picked one, rolled it, and in-

serted it in the empty bottle's neck. She arranged the bottles on a windowsill and sometimes photographed them in
various lights, telling herself she was working.

When the envelopes stopped coming with any regular-
ity—weeks passed between packages, then months—she
began to believe her ordeal was over. She felt her ability to
work return, threw away the bottles, opened a new one, and
left it full on the sill as a sign of liberation. Then another package appeared in her mailbox. She had been venturing out
with her camera, and this new batch spooked her. Cold suddenly, she returned to her apartment and wrapped herself
in her terry robe and sat by the window until the afternoon
light faded, trying to interest herself in the view, not wanting to think about the photographs.

But she spread them on the kitchen table anyway. One was
of her sitting in the bathtub, naked, her breasts glistening, a
hand squeezing water from a washcloth above them onto one
erect nipple, like an off-center bull's-eye on her chest. The
tub water circled her waist. Something about her hair caught
her attention.

She bent closer to study the photograph but couldn't quite
place what was bothering her—other than that the photograph even existed—what caused a warning bell to go off in
her mind like a distant car alarm. Frustrated, she shuffled the
photographs together and threw them back on the table.
How had Spadafore gotten the photograph? Her apartment
was on the twenty-second floor. The window washers. But
she couldn't remember them ever being outside her window
while she bathed. Still, the focus was odd, as if the camera
had been pressed against glass for the picture.

She was shivering. She checked the thermostat, paced, stood in her bare feet by a heater, poured some wine, spilling it on the table and photos. She scooped them up, grabbed her wineglass, and went into the bedroom to search through the other pictures. She had boxes of them stacked against the wall. For over an hour she looked, putting the coffee-colored envelopes on her bed and leafing through their contents. Nothing clicked. She stood, stretched her back, saw her face in a mirror. Then she knew why the bathtub photograph bothered her.

She found it again. Her hair was longer. In the picture, curls hung from twin barrettes, reaching halfway down her arms. She sat on the bed, her legs folding beneath her like coiled rope.

When had her hair last been like that? 1985? It couldn't have been after '87. The picture came from half a decade ago, years before she'd even contracted Spadafore. She lay down and rolled over to look at the picture from a different angle and stared at it so long the image began to blur and dissolve. She lay curled on her bed in the darkened room, rocking slightly, damp photographs clinging to her robe and skin, herself herself herself.

B OXES

All night I didn't sleep. My shins were bruised and my throat tasted bloody and I kept remembering Willie holding my mouth open under the faucet, saying I had a week to get his seventeen hundred dollars. I lay on the bed sweating from the heat, a baseball bat beside me, afraid that he'd come back. In the first blue blur of day I could see the calendar tacked to my wall: the months crossed off in different colors, the days I'd exercised boxed in black. For nearly a year I'd been straight and then Willie showed up, telling me I had to pay this debt. I'd worried this might happen since my days in the halfway house and now that it had, the question was, what was I going to do about it?

The sun rose, striping the pavement between houses with shafts of yellow light and turning the tree leaves an almost transparent green. Willie wouldn't be out now: he did his work by night. I rolled off the bed and looked in the mirror. My eyes were pink and sunken and a red weal circled my throat. It was still tender, and I pulled on a turtleneck to hide it. I pushed the chair away from the door and stepped into the kitchen, where broken plates lay scattered over the counter and chairs and black coffee was pooled in the shards of a yellow cup. "I hear you went straight," Willie had said, folding his knife away. I nodded, looking up at him from the floor, holding my bruised legs. I couldn't see his eyes because his face was hidden by the hooded sweatshirt. He never liked people to look at him. He picked up one of the plates I'd bought at a discount store and inspected it. "Lots of good it done you," he said, and smashed the plate on the counter. He moved to the door kicking debris aside and paused in the frame, filling it like a huge albino cork. "You'll be back," he said, and left.

The remains of last night's dinner were still on the table— a neat pyramid of chicken bones and a hunk of good bread, some lettuce and a green bottle of olive oil—the only part of the room that didn't look like a train wreck. I'd had my first cookout. After eating I sat for a while in the dim, cool room with the last of the day's sunlight high up on the walls, enjoying the taste of grilled chicken and olive oil lingering in my mouth. For a long time I'd gone without such simple pleasures, and the world had felt bled dry of color and taste. This was one of the first times they seemed to be coming back.

I had gone for a walk in the early dark before cleaning up and when I returned there was a new smell in the apartment, a tangy mixture of sweat and weed. It was familiar but not immediately so, as if it came from someone else's past that I had heard about and not my own. By the time I realized it was Willie he'd grabbed a fistful of my hair and smashed my face against the counter. Most of the rest of the beating blurred over.

I couldn't eat in the kitchen now; just looking at the sink made my throat ache. I decided to get something on the way to work.

I turned the key in the ignition and nothing happened. I kept pushing until the key dug into my palm and the engine began to turn over, slowly. I had about seven hundred dollars in my account, saved up from six weeks' work. That left me nearly a thousand short. If I sold the car I couldn't get to work, and besides, I'd be lucky to get five hundred for it since the electrical system was shot. I floored the accelerator and put the car in gear and backed out the driveway over some branches, which scraped against the undercarriage, wondering if Herb still worked at the bank. He might write me a loan. I doubted it, but I didn't have many options.

I got to work early. Creech and Gortney and a few others were hanging around the Dumpster in the back of the lot, drinking coffee. They wouldn't wave hello. I'd been costing them a lot of money, not going along with their system; before I started working they each used to make an extra few thousand a year stealing TVs. When I drove up Gortney dumped his coffee on the gravel and headed into the warehouse, his shirt already untucked.

Stepping out of the car was like having someone wrap me in a hot damp towel: the heat clung to my skin. The side of the warehouse glowed white in the sun, and I had to look away. I ducked inside through a small door cut into the larger, rolling one, and my stomach clenched from the paint and diesel fumes. I always noticed them first thing in the morning, then forgot about them until the next day, which seemed to define my life recently. I needed to relearn the same lessons almost daily, to be patient, to be responsible, to eat well, to not dwell on the past. At least, that's what I'd been thinking until Willie reappeared. Now, I wasn't so sure what I was supposed to learn.

The air inside felt cool, almost chilly, but it wouldn't stay that way for long. By eleven, with the sun beating on the tin roof, we'd all be baking. Reemer, my foreman, stood by the clock, gripping his clipboard. He smelled faintly of talc. "You look like shit," he said.

"Everyone has their days." I punched in, the puncher echoing like a shot in the quiet warehouse. I didn't want to talk but I didn't want to make Reemer nervous either so I caught his gaze and held it to show I wasn't coked up. He knew Jones had hired me under special circumstances, though just how much he knew I wasn't sure.

"Someone give you a hickey?" He pointed his tagger at my neck. "No other reason to wear a turtleneck in this weather than a hickey."

"I had a wild night." I poked his shoulder. "You couldn't guess the half of it."

I headed down an aisle of stacked boxes to Reemer's office. Outside the door, in a blue tray, were the day's work orders. There weren't any trucks in the loading docks yet but I could get started anyway, shifting boxes onto pallets and then moving the pallets up the concrete ramps with a forklift. Reemer followed me from the clock. I sorted through the orders, aware that he was watching me, then set to work. It was mindless labor, but I was glad to have it. I ached all over from the beating Willie gave me and if I had time to think about it I'd probably get scared.

My job was to count the boxes twice, first when I put them on the pallets and then again with the trucking foreman, and once we agreed on the count we signed the shipping forms together. That way, no one could put extra boxes on the truck to sell on his own. At least theoretically. If I cheated and the trucking foreman cheated, we could put down whatever number we wanted and sell the rest, which is exactly what Creech and Gortney had been doing for years. That's why Reemer gave me this job; he didn't trust either Creech or Gortney but couldn't fire them on suspicion, and they were too careful to get caught. From time to time Reemer took over the loading, but he had too many other jobs to pay close attention to this one for long.

"Every one of these boxes is yours," Reemer had said when I'd first started working. He rested his big palm on a box gently, as if it were the head of a child. "Make sure you don't lose any."

I recognized the "God and country" speech. I'd given plenty like it to workers when I owned my own company, and it had always embarrassed me, but I found it strangely reassuring to be on the receiving end, a sign that I had a defined place in the world when for so long I had been floating. I also liked that Reemer trusted me. He was the first one in months.

I set to work, counting, shifting, lifting. After an hour and a half I had two trucks' worth of pallets stacked and waiting, close to a thousand boxes. Winded, I rested my head against one stack and breathed in the dusty smell of the cardboard. It's not something you'd ever think you'd get attached to, but I had. I looked forward to going to work each day and smelling the smells of work, especially this one. Sometimes I raked my thumbnail down a box just to bring it out more. There were other things I'd come to like, too: the way I fell asleep each night within minutes of going to bed, the soreness in my shoulders at the end of each day. I felt as if I'd been strapped to a harness, and it was a satisfying type of ache. Willie's wasn't, and thinking of him I shuddered.

Creech whistled to get my attention and waved to let me know they were ready to load, and I nodded and sped toward him on the forklift. He headed into the dark interior of a trailer, disappearing so quickly and so completely it was like he'd fallen down a hole.

I shifted the lift's arms into place, picked up the first pallet, and bumped slowly off the ramp into the trailer, where Creech and Gortney were waiting for me in the dark. The engine's rumble echoed in the hollow interior so that it sounded like a fleet of lifts was following me even though I knew I was alone. I wasn't sure how far to go and I went slowly until I picked out the pale shine of Creech's bald spot near the back wall. The first two times I'd driven into a darkened truck I lost my sense of direction and crashed into the sides. Creech and Gortney had imitated me for days, swerving their lifts like they were drunk, then nicknamed me Amelia Earhart. Now, their dim figures were darker shad-

ows in the dark until my eyes grew accustomed to the light
and their features emerged, as if they were being molded
while I came closer.

Gortney had a thin, sharp face and small black eyes and a
stiff mustache; he looked as if his mother had mated with a
rat. Creech had a body like a Chicano car, a real low-rider.
Both of them were still giving me the silent treatment and I
maneuvered the pallet into the far corner without waiting
for directions.

Their silence went back to the end of my first week, when
Creech had asked me to put some extra boxes on a truck. I
wouldn't. I didn't know what he meant at first, though he
thought I was just playing dumb. "What?" I said. "I can't. I
have to count every one."

"So miss one. It's worth twenty-five bucks to you, every
time." Creech counted the boxes, running his hands over
them like they were melons. Somehow, I couldn't bear to
watch him touch them, and I pushed them just out of his
reach.

Gortney slapped me on the back. "Come on, Amelia. It's
a cardboard box. In the course of a lifetime, who's going to
miss a few?"

When I realized what Creech meant I just stared at him,
then continued loading. I counted each box out loud and let
it drop with a thud. Somehow Reemer found out about it,
because he shook my hand at the end of the day and Gortney saw it. I knew Gortney and Creech thought I blew them
in, but I didn't care. Later, Reemer told me Creech and
Gortney had flipped everybody who'd held my job, and then
turned two of them in—to make it look like they weren't

the ones doing the stealing. Once I knew that, I was even gladder I hadn't listened to them.

I goosed the throttle to disengage the sticky lift, and Creech looked up at the sound. Even knowing they might turn on me, I thought now of asking if they still wanted help running their scam. Willie was serious about what I owed him, and he'd been tried once for murder. A witness said Willie had brought another dealer out a deserted road to the salt marshes, shot him through the ear, tied weights around his ankles and wrists, and then rowed out to dump the body in the tall weeds. None of the jurors believed the other guy. He had come forward eight years later, and without a body. But after last night, I was willing to believe anything about Willie, and rolling the dice with Creech and Gortney seemed a lot less deadly.

Still, I thought my best bet would be the bank. I shifted to reverse, the warning bell sounding, backed the lift out, and turned and headed for another pallet stacked on the ramp, listening as I left to the rising murmur of Creech and Gortney's voices. Loading took half an hour. They didn't speak to me once.

Just before lunch Reemer grabbed my arm as I went by and yanked me into his office.

"What's up, Johnson?" He closed the door, thinking he was being inconspicuous.

I rubbed my neck to let him know I didn't think his method was the smoothest, but he didn't seem to notice. He leaned forward and looked me over as if he were waiting for me to start tweaking at any moment, which just showed how little he really knew about drugs. Cocaine cravings aren't like that. Your mouth gets dry and your stomach cramps and feels heavy, like you've swallowed a fruitcake whole, but no one else can tell. If I really wanted some blow I probably wouldn't look this bad. Besides, I was too scared to want anything but money.

"Nothing," I said, but I couldn't meet his eyes. I looked at the small desk overflowing with papers, the notices pinned to the corkboard walls, the knuckled glass windows crossed by steel bars. The light coming through the windows was dim, like we were under water.

"You can tell me." Reemer laid his hand on my shoulder. The skin on his knuckles was cracked and scabbed. It looked painful, but I'd never seen him shirking. Someone in the company once told me Reemer's hands would bleed for weeks on end in the winter. "I know it must be hard for you."

I thought about it for a long time. Reemer's voice was understanding and his face seemed honest, but I remembered Jones, his boss, when I interviewed. My counselor sat with a file in her lap—my recommendations from the halfway house and from my other counselors—and Jones stood by a window, rising up on the balls of his feet and then dropping down on his heels while he thought it over. I watched his heels going up and down, knowing that my chances rode on how he finally decided: up, down, up, down, the physical manifestation of his mental gymnastics. I had done a lot to bring myself to this point, good things recently and bad ones before, but the decision now was out of my hands.

Finally he came down for a last time, harder than the others, as if he'd reached his decision and meant to seal the lid on it with his heels. In one quick glance he took me in, then turned to Carol and said, "All right." He kept talking to Carol, as if he were a teacher addressing my parent. "But if his past comes into work in any way, he's gone."

He sat down and began signing papers. He didn't shake my hand. I couldn't blame him. For all the recommendations I had in the folder there were other papers, accounts of what I'd done or of how much I'd fallen in debt or of how I'd run a business into the ground, and there was the sentencing report too, where the judge said he didn't agree with the plea bargain because he didn't believe I'd really changed, but was bound to go along with it.

How could I explain to Reemer that I owed seventeen hundred dollars to my ex-dealer? I wasn't supposed to go near him, and I hadn't, but nobody would understand that. They'd fire me and I'd never get another job and the judge would revoke my probation.

I tried to think of a lie to tell Reemer but decided that wouldn't work, either. I'd gotten out of the habit since I went straight and I didn't really want to take it up again, especially with Reemer, and even if I thought of one I wasn't sure I could pull it off. I read from a list of regulations posted on the wall. NO SPEEDING ON THE FORKLIFT. NO SWEARING ON THE FORKLIFT. NO JOUSTING WITH THE FORKLIFTS. Those were all because of Creech. NO SLACKING. That was probably directed at Gortney, but I doubted he'd ever bothered to read it. NO DRUGS! That one was mine.

"It's nothing, really," I said. "Sometimes I just have sleepless nights, you know?"

That was true enough, as far as it went, and it seemed to

satisfy Reemer. He stared at me unblinking, the skin under his eyes shiny with sweat in the heat. This time I looked back until a ledger slid off a pile of papers, startling me. Finally he nodded.

"Okay. Just make sure that's all it is."

"I have to leave early this afternoon," I said, before he could tell me to go. "On business." I didn't think he'd mind since I'd never asked before, but when he didn't say anything I added, "It's important to me."

"Two-thirty okay?" He flipped a page over the back of his clipboard and studied the next one. "You should be done your orders by then."

"That's fine."

"Good." He ran his pen down the line of names printed under the schedule, and I started to go.

"And Johnson."

I turned around, holding on to the door. I knew what he was going to say: this job was my last chance. How could he think I didn't know?

He wrote something next to one of the names and then spoke without looking up, the pen poised above the paper. "You're doing good work. I tell Mr. Jones that every week."

I thanked him and walked outside. Everybody was play- ing touch football in the parking lot, where heat waves shim- mered on the pavement. Sitting out as I always did, I watched from the concrete loading dock, my legs dangling over the rubber bumper, the warm breeze trailing around my throat.

Before I left I grabbed an empty box from the Dumpster and threw it in my trunk. Willie had broken so many things in

my apartment that all of them wouldn't fit into my trash
cans. Creech and Gortney stopped pushing boxes around to
look when they saw me drive off. I'd rinsed my face and
hands in the bathroom sink and toweled off under my arms,
wanting to appear employed but not filthy, and they probably thought I had some kind of date. I hoped the hour might
make Herb more expansive.

It didn't. He was not happy to see me. I hadn't called
ahead, not wanting to give him the option of refusing me over
the phone, so I just walked by his secretary when she came
out of his office for a file. She hurried after me saying, "Sir,
sir," but Herb told her it was all right.

Herb had small blue eyes made larger by round rimless
glasses, and a probing gaze I found unsettling even at my best.
Now, I had trouble withstanding it. He seemed to be calling up all my sins and marching them before his eyes one by
one for review, but I knew he wasn't. That would take too
long.

"Take a seat," he said finally, and I obeyed.

I got right to it. "I need a thousand dollars." I sat forward
on the couch. I could feel my legs sweating, even with the
air-conditioning, sticking to my khakis.

"So do I," he said. He didn't smile.

"No." I dismissed the joke with my hand. "You don't understand. I really need it. Badly."

"I thought you'd kicked the habit, though I have to say
you'd never know it." He shifted a pen from one corner of
his bare blotter to another. "You look almost like you did two
years ago."

"I'm clean. That's not what I need it for."

"Buying a house?"

"I'm not buying anything. I'm paying off old debts."

"Yes." He opened and closed a desk drawer repeatedly, letting it bounce against his stomach and then click shut. "You must have plenty of those."

"Just this one. When it's paid off, I won't have any others."

I realized that sounded like a lot of my promises from before I quit the stuff, about how I was going to change, and I had the urge to get up and pace. I forced myself to remain still and decided to be honest. "I have to pay off my old dealer. When I went into treatment I still owed him money. He's not the kind to forget it. That's why I look this way." Herb didn't say anything, so I kept talking. "I've got a job. You can check it out. Use my pay as collateral. A thousand isn't that much. It'll be paid off in no time, maybe four months."

"So tell the cops."

"I can't." I looked at the pictures Herb had of himself on the walls. There used to be some of the two of us together, playing ball, fishing, but they were gone. Discolored paint marked the places they'd once hung. I'd hoped to draw some strength from them. "I mean it won't do any good. He's beaten plenty of raps before, and to be honest, I don't think I could stand the pressure of a trial." I forced a laugh. "I'm not sure I'd survive that long anyway."

Herb shifted his gaze to the back of his door. I listened to the quiet whooshing of air being forced into the office and counted off the seconds on my fingers. My thumbs were growing broader from work; my fingertips and palms were callused. I'd reached ninety before Herb took a deep breath and started to speak.

"I'm not going to loan you anything, and I'll tell you why. I don't think you're ready for it." He sat forward so abruptly I thought he was going to come over the desk after me. "You say you've only got one debt, which means you don't realize the full extent of some of the things you've done." He reached into his drawer and pulled out a sheaf of papers. "See these?" He shook them once, as if they were letters he'd received against me. "They're files about people I have to see next week. You know what I do now? Foreclosures." He let the word hang. "I repossess things—cars, boats, motorcycles, that kind of stuff. Young kids can't pay their bills, or a family overextends itself? I'm the one who shows up to remind them. All because I went to bat for you for a long time."

He put the papers back in the drawer and shoved the drawer closed. I expected him to sigh and rub his hands over his face, but he sat perfectly still, his hands fisted on the desk. He seemed to be making an effort to control himself, as if he might shake apart at any instant. "I don't like this job. If you walked in here with a million dollars in gold as collateral, I wouldn't loan you thirty cents.

"But, here." He pulled out his wallet and lay a crisp twenty on the desk, then pushed it across the blotter with his fingertips. "For old times." He adjusted his glasses with both hands.

I knew he meant the twenty dollars as an insult. "Okay," I said. I wanted to hit him, I wanted to apologize for all I'd done before, I wanted to say I missed the times we'd spent together, but he didn't care anymore what I wanted, and bringing up any of it would only be self-indulgent. "Thanks for your time." I left the money on the desk and walked out.

Outside, still sweating, I could feel myself starting to gag in the heat. I rolled down all the windows to let the car cool off and sat at the wheel, the door open, head in my hands. I thought of my mother. I couldn't go see her. When I was in the halfway house she wouldn't even come to family counseling sessions. I'd taken her savings and said I was investing it while blowing it up my nose. That's what I'd put aside the seven hundred for; I was going to try and pay her back. I knew it wasn't much, but when it got to a couple thousand I thought maybe I'd show up with it, see if the money couldn't be a start. I heard she was working again, waiting tables.

I decided to try another bank. There were two more on the same street and I went into both. The loan officers at each were very polite, well dressed, shook hands firmly. Neither wanted to lend me a penny.

Back at the apartment I swept up everything—plates, cups, glasses—whether it was broken or not, and threw it in the box. The food on the table went too, greasy and stale-smelling, and a stool with one leg split neatly in half. Done, I leaned on the broom in a corner, looking the apartment over. I saw dingy paint, doors and windows that were out of plumb, floors that still seemed dirty, and I wondered if I'd always feel that way no matter how much I swept and scrubbed. I decided to skip my Monday night meeting, which I knew wasn't healthy, but I was too worn out to care. I took a steamy shower, popping my head out from behind the curtain every few seconds to listen for strange noises, then shifted the bureau in front of the door with the box propped on the edge of it. If I dozed off and Willie pushed on the door I'd hear the box fall and have a few seconds' warning. When I lay down on the bed, I was holding the bat again.

A thunderstorm came and went, the thunder rattling my windows, the rain sounding like a mass of people marching on the street. Afterward, the air blowing in through the screen was cool and smelled of damp grass. I listened to passing cars, their wheels shushing through puddles, and to the sounds of kids shouting to one other as they played in the dark, and to my own quickened breathing. For a long time I was too wired to fall asleep, so I wrestled with myself about what to do.

I thought of Jones, his back turned for the longest time, and of Reemer, who I wanted to please. And I thought of my time in the center, begging for drugs at first and then feeling cured, and then corkscrewing into a long depression where I once decided, If this is what it's like to be off coke, why bother? It lifted only gradually. Then came the halfway house. Some of the guys didn't last: they returned drunk after work or didn't return at all. The rest of us were scared but wanted more than anything to make it. I almost had, and if I could get rid of Willie and his knife I believed I would. A thousand dollars would let me.

I tried to remember who might owe me money, places I might have stashed some a year or two before, if anyone at the halfway house was rich. I pictured different accidents happening to Willie—a car crash, an overdose, an aneurysm erupting during a pickup basketball game, him choking on

his own fat tongue. I thought of asking Reemer, but I didn't
know him half as well as I knew Herb and look where that
had gotten me. Of course, Reemer's relative unfamiliarity
with my history might be a plus; still, I knew the thought was
a pipe dream. Who was going to hand a recovering addict a
thousand dollars to give his ex-dealer? Nobody.

What was it that Gortney had said? In the course of a lifetime, who'd miss a few boxes? He was probably right. As-
suming for a minute that Gortney and Creech would go
along with me, I did some math. At twenty-five dollars a box,
seven hundred and fifty dollars meant six boxes a day for five
days. My savings brought it to fourteen-fifty, and my next
paycheck, since it was for two weeks, would put me over
the top. I wouldn't eat much until I got paid again but that
didn't bother me. Not getting the money would.

I kept coming back to Creech and Gortney turning in
people who were their source of cash. It must be about more
than the money for them: making the money while keeping
Reemer and Jones off balance, beating the system by playing the game better than anyone gave them credit for—
those must have been the real attractions. No wonder they
were so angry at me. Until I said yes, they couldn't even
enter play. If I did, I'd let them think I was serving both our
purposes, but I could go along with them just long enough
to get the money I needed and then pull out, before they had
a chance to do me in.

I sat up and looked at the box on my bureau and the idea's
appeal faded. The plan was too complex and risky and,
worse, in its workings I could see my old life rushing up to
swallow me whole: stealing and lying, trading the singular

trouble of Willie for two more in Creech and Gortney, all in an attempt to straighten out a situation crooked from the start. I didn't want to plow that field again. Soon the troubles would reproduce like monkeys, filling up my days, chattering at me constantly about what I owed and why and how I had to do this or that to pay them off, and that could end only in some disaster, as it had the last time. I remembered my mother turning away from me in her kitchen, saying there were some debts I could never repay. Creech and Gortney would be another one—they'd hold those thirty boxes over me forever, threatening to turn me in if I didn't steal more, then doing it when they got tired of me. And if Reemer discovered it, it would be like I was looking into my mother's disappointed face all over again.

No, I had to find a better way, some method of getting Creech and Gortney to pay me for the trouble I was going to go through, some kind of indemnity. As soon as I thought that word—*indemnity*—I felt something click, and I knew it was how I could do this. They'd have to prove that they weren't going to flip me. I checked the clock. Three A.M. I rolled over, punched my pillow into shape, and closed my eyes. I'd talk to Creech first thing in the morning.

I threw the box in my trunk and drove to work as the sun came up, going over the figures, twisting the radio dial restlessly, and honking at slow starters at every light. My stomach was growling—I hadn't eaten in a day and a half—and sweat was beginning under my arms; my legs and throat still ached. I wanted to get the thing started but I was so nervous I missed the warehouse entrance first time by.

I turned back and headed up the driveway, gravel crunching beneath my tires. Creech was joking with some of the drivers out by the swamp willows. I sat in my car watching them laugh and pass around a thermos. Gortney drove in behind me and joined them and when Creech looked up I waved. He turned away. I took a deep breath, fished around under my seat until I found a plastic mug, and walked over. It seemed to take forever. I remembered the twelve steps. I heard some bragging about fishing: secret trout holes up on the Black River; who tied the best flies. When I joined the group everyone stopped talking.

"Hi," I felt like saying. "My name's Kevin and I'm a drug addict," but they wouldn't have gotten the joke. I nodded to Creech and Gortney and Smith, one of the drivers. The others I didn't recognize. No one nodded back. It seemed like I'd interrupted a joke just before the punch line and they were waiting for me to leave to tell it.

I held my mug toward Creech, who had the thermos. "Can I have a cup?" My voice broke, like I was going through puberty, but I managed to keep my hand from shaking.

"Get lost, Amelia," Gortney said. He spit near my shoes.

Creech ignored him. "Sure." When he poured, steam swirled around his thick wrist.

"Can I talk to you a minute?" I said, loud enough for him to hear, quiet enough that I hoped the others wouldn't.

He raised his eyebrows and smiled, passed the thermos to Gortney.

We stepped away. Sticks broke under my feet, and I heard a crow cawing in the trashy field behind us.

I drank some of the coffee. "We talked before about some

business," I started. I had to clear my throat. "Still interested?"

"Maybe."

I could tell he was. He rotated his shoulders in such a way. My eyes felt like they were bulging out of my head; the coffee scalded my tongue.

"How do you normally work it? Cash at the end of the day?"

"If you want it that way." He squatted down and scooped up a handful of gravel. "That's a bit trickier." He seemed to be inspecting the gravel in his cupped palm. He turned the stones over one at a time with his thumbnail, which looked abnormally white against the gray stones.

"Doesn't have to be," I said. "I'll go somewhere to meet you."

"Okay." He closed his fist over the gravel, rattled it, and tossed it away.

"Just how much money are we talking here?" I said. "I mean, is this really going to be worthwhile for me?"

"Four, maybe five thousand a year," he said.

"I'll make that much?"

"No. We will. You'll make a lot less. One. Two if it's a good year."

I squatted beside him. He'd gotten a little carried away, trying to impress me, which was good. It gave me an opening. "For taking all the risk."

"Hardly. Anyone can miscount. That's what you tell Reemer if he catches you. Us?" He looked around, as if someone might be listening, then began digging channels in the gravel with his fingers. "We're the ones holding property that's not ours. No. Twenty-five dollars a box is just about right."

"Well how much do the TVs bring?"

"Each?" His lips moved while he calculated. "Two hundred dollars."

"Bull. A Trinitron retails for fifteen hundred."

"You don't get retail on the street."

"You don't get soaked that much, either. So at least four hundred."

He cracked a slight grin, which he covered quickly by coughing and standing. "Why now?" he said. "Why didn't you go for this before?"

I stood too, shifted my weight from one foot to the other, and faced him. Anybody watching was going to think we were playing a bizarre variation of leap-frog. "It was too soon after I got here. What was it, a week after they hired me? I didn't trust you. I thought you were setting me up."

"And now you've just decided to be a nice guy and help us out."

I had to be careful about what I said next. I needed him to believe me, but I didn't want to tell him so much he'd have me in a weakened position. "Let's just say I could use some money."

"Sure," he said, nodding, as if to convince himself. "Everyone gets hard up now and again."

"That's right. But Reemer told me you've blown in a couple of guys for this scam."

"I wouldn't trust Reemer too far."

"I don't trust anybody. That's why I'm asking for some proof."

"How much?" His voice was so flat it was hard to tell he'd asked a question.

"Four hundred." I might as well have some extra.

"That's a lot of money."

He said it too quickly, and I knew he didn't mean it. "Not really."

"We might be able to do that."

"Each. You, Gortney, and the driver."

"No way."

"Two-fifty then. And that's my last offer."

He was silent. The wind snapped a blue plastic bag caught in a tree and Creech glanced up at it flapping in the branches. I was sure he was going to say no.

"A box a truck, six trucks a day. You guys will have the money you've fronted me back in two days. And you'll make it back anyway by selling two TVs."

"That's too fast. The most we do is every other truck, and that's only during the Christmas rush." His arms were still folded.

"Look. Don't pay me another cent until after we're even," I said, hurrying. I didn't want to appear to be giving away too much, but I had to hook him. "I won't raise my rate for a year. Twenty-five bucks a pop—that's nothing. Consider it a down payment. Thirty boxes' worth."

He still didn't bite. I'd been counting on their greed, but maybe I'd overestimated it. I was considering lowering my demand one last time, since even five hundred from them might be enough, when he sniffled and lowered his chin to his chest, then dropped his arms. I knew I had him. I was always good at negotiations—now I just had to not blow it.

"All right," I said, making it seem like I was giving in. "We can do a truck every other day, for all I care. You'll still get your money's worth."

He scuffed the toe of his boot through the gravel. "You're asking me to give you seven hundred and fifty dollars for nothing."

"No. I'm asking you to give me the money so I know you're serious. I like this job. I need it. And I need the extra money. That ought to be enough to convince you right there. But what I need more than anything is to know you're for real, not setting me up. The money will prove that."

He pursed his lips.

"Pluses and minuses, Frank," I said, using his name for the first time, which caused him to look at me. "That's what everything comes down to, and if you don't realize this is a plus, well . . ." I opened my hands, palms up, to indicate that if he didn't get it he was a fool.

"If we front you this money—and that's a big if—it's only after you've given us the first box. We need some safe-guards, too."

"Okay, sure." I wanted to make it sound like I was think-ing it over. "That's reasonable. Let's do a Trinitron right off the bat. We'll be just about even."

Creech shrugged. "What the hell. I'll ask. Hold on. I'll check it out with the others."

"No." I grabbed his sleeve, which surprised him. "I don't want Reemer to see me talking to you."

He turned to say something and his face had a keen, feral expression I hadn't seen before. I pulled back and wiped my hand on my pants. Creech noticed it.

"Hand dirty?" Creech said.

I started to say something, but Creech cut me off. "You came to me, remember. This great scheme was your idea, not mine. So if we decide to do it, you better get used to the way I feel. I'm going to be your goddamn body glove."

A plane flew low overhead and its noise shook the ground. Creech started to walk away and then came back and stood so close to me that I could smell the coffee on his breath. "Next time you get a bright idea don't be so stupid and approach me like this. You can bet your boyfriend Reemer has been watching this whole thing."

When he turned and walked toward the warehouse, blindingly white in the morning sun, Gortney went with him, hunching down to whisper while looking at me over his shoulder. Sure enough, I saw Reemer's face framed in the small door's window, and when Creech and Gortney went in he stepped halfway out so I would see him.

"Don't be late," Reemer called, then slammed the door shut behind him.

I thought about leaving. Why not? It looked like I'd blown my last chance. I saw myself driving on long open roads behind the wheel of my car, the miles ticking away, but I knew it was a fantasy, as the belief had been that I could somehow escape my old life, and since I didn't have anywhere else to turn, I went in.

"Hi!" Reemer said, right in my ear.

I dropped the mug and splashed coffee on my thigh. "Christ, Reemer," I said, pulling the wet pants away from my skin. "It's too early for that." I shook my leg like a dog.

"Too early for a lot of things," Reemer said, tapping a thick finger on the door window. He clucked his tongue as if he were disappointed in me. "I didn't figure you as the type to deal with slimeballs."

"I'm not."

"Then what were you doing out there?"

"I don't have any deal, all right?"

I was breathing hard, and my words came out with such conviction that he was unsure what to do next. Before he could start up again I pushed by him and turned down a row of shelves toward his office. I didn't have a deal. What he didn't know was how much I wished I did.

I knew if I went to Creech again I'd never get my money, so I waited—three days—but it wasn't easy. I didn't eat much; I rarely slept; when my phone rang I didn't answer it. At work I avoided everyone, especially Reemer, who seemed suspicious of me. Thursday afternoon I stacked a wall of pallets and boxes next to the loading ramp. The boxes had been dropped off outside that morning, left by all our parked cars, since the shipping bay was temporarily full. I had to put them somewhere sheltered and somewhere people couldn't easily pick them up and toss them in their cars, but when I explained all that to Reemer he shook his head and said, "I can't see trucks from my office now."

"So what?"

"So this makes it easier to steal."

"You're paranoid, Al."

"I'm paid to be paranoid."

He watched me go in and out of the warehouse every few

loads, leaning against the doorjamb with his clipboard. I could see his head nod as he counted the boxes.

Creech brushed against me, mouthed the words "This truck," and passed by. He was so inconspicuous that I wasn't even sure it had happened, but I couldn't very well ask him, and since I only had forty-eight hours before Willie's return I didn't bother.

He and Gortney looked at me as I came in with each load, but I kept my eyes straight ahead and didn't speak to either of them. Halfway through the truck, I went back to the office and flipped through the order forms again, standing so Reemer could see me. He was at his desk. I waited for him to look up, but he wouldn't. He checked items on his clipboard, slowly, and when he reached the bottom of the page he started over at the top. I could hear the pen scratching over the paper. He never took that much time.

I walked toward the forklift, snapping a rubber band on my wrist, my fingers sticky with sweat, then whirred across the floor to the base of the ramp, where I stopped to fill out the numbers on the slip. I re-counted the TVs without looking around and paused before signing it. When I did I caught a whiff of talc. I was glad to see my signature wasn't too shaky.

Reemer clapped me on the shoulder. "Are you going to do the work or not?" he said. "There's twenty boxes on this pallet."

"I can count."

"I can, too. What's it say on that form?" He took it from my hand.

"Twenty."

It did, but he studied it so long he seemed to expect the number to change in front of him. "Well what are you waiting for?" he said finally, handing it back. "Get going."

I fired the forklift up and moved off so quickly the load wobbled and nearly toppled. I put it in the truck, shifted into reverse, and started backing out. Over the warning bell I said to Creech, "All set," and then drove off. When I came back with the next load Creech and Gortney were waiting on the ramp. Creech met me halfway, the first time that had happened since I turned him down months before. It took a few seconds before I figured out what he was after: serving notice that they were the ones in control and that I'd better watch myself or they'd make the scam so obvious I'd get fired. Reemer was bound to be suspicious of him giving me help.

I zipped by him into the truck, which smelled sweetly of onions, the last thing to be carried in it. A few papery skins littered the floor and they swirled away at my approach. When I came over the hump, Gortney leaned his rat face into the cage and for a second I thought he was going to kiss me.

"Glad to do business with you, Amelia," he said, slapping me on the back.

Creech trotted up behind us. "Welcome aboard." He made it sound as if I'd joined a pirate ship. I moved away and drove to the back without stopping, then idled the engine and awaited their approach. The truck floor rocked beneath their steps. Gortney, always the more practical of the two, began counting the load. When he was done he started over again, then smacked the last box in irritation.

"I told you we couldn't trust him," he said to Frank. "There's only twenty on this load, too."

Creech looked at me.

"Let me see the envelope."

"That wasn't the deal."

"It is now. Just let me see it."

Gortney was watching Creech, who tilted his head as a sign of approval. Gortney opened his jacket and I saw the top of a thick white envelope sticking out of his inside pocket.

"Check the load before the last one."

"It's buried."

"So it's harder to spot. Count them if you want to."

"Christ," Gortney muttered, but he started scrambling over the boxes to get at the others.

We waited. When we heard him again his voice was muffled by the stacked boxes.

"He's right."

"Just in case Reemer counted this load," I said.

Gortney dropped down beside me.

"Amelia! You're a regular fox. We're going to have to give you a new nickname."

"Save the name. I want my money." If I didn't get it right now, I wouldn't get it at all.

"We could turn you in for what you just did."

"Forget it, Creech. You're bluffing. I'm not. Give it to me or I'll blow the whole deal."

They exchanged glances. "I mean it," I said, and I did. If I was going down, I'd be happy to take them with me.

Creech sucked his teeth. "Okay," he said, nodding at Gort-

ney, who blew a disgusted sigh. He shook his head, but
pulled out the envelope and slapped it into my palm.

"You're smart, Frank," I said. "Letting Gortney carry like
that."

"Fuck you."

"Get the Trinitron box," I said. "There's only one. You'll
earn back half your money."

The envelope was so white it seemed fluorescent. It felt
heavy, and even though I had been right about their greed
and their desire to run the scam, I still didn't trust them.

"If this is short, you've gotten your last box."

I knew I should resist trying to count it, but I couldn't.
Just as I opened it and began thumbing the bills I heard bang-
ing and Reemer's voice, shouting. "What the hell is going
on down there?" He was back in the rectangle of light at the
end of the truck, pounding on the sidewall with his open
palm, the blows reverberating around us.

I stashed the envelope and whispered, "Let me handle
this."

Then louder, I said, "No, you're the asshole!" to Gortney,
and swung.

He saw my fist coming and lurched back, trying to get out
of the way, but succeeded only in giving me a different tar-
get. I'd been going for his nose and ended up connecting with
his Adam's apple, which felt hard and sharp as a brick. He
toppled over backward, making odd gagging noises, and I
said to Creech, "Sorry. I had to. Now get this truck out of
here before Reemer recounts it."

I started out toward Reemer, trying to shake the pain from
my hand.

He led me to his office, shut the door, told me to sit down. He stood above me.

"Are you trying to get your ass fired?"

"No sir." I rubbed my knuckles.

"Because you're doing a good job of it."

"We won't have any problems like that again. Believe me. I straightened the whole thing out."

"We better not." I knew he'd seen the punch, and that probably disposed him in my favor. He'd never liked Gortney. Still, he didn't seem to believe that a fight was the only thing going on. I would have liked to tell him the truth, but what I really wanted was to go somewhere and count the money.

"Did you put an extra box on that truck?"

"I haven't lied to you, Al."

"You didn't answer my question."

"I didn't put an extra TV on that truck."

We had a staring match. I wasn't going to back down.

"I could go out there and pull every box off and match its number with the manifests."

"Go right ahead." I didn't hesitate. He'd know something was up. "I'll help you." I pulled my gloves back on, stretched out my fingers.

He started to say something—I heard the sharp intake of his breath, his mouth opened to form sounds, and I thought he was going to ask about the envelope, which would be tricky since I didn't have any ready reply—but then the time clock clunked as it reached the hour. Reemer's eyes shifted to it, and the distraction gave him an excuse to dismiss me.

"Go," he said, reaching around me to open the door. "And

cut out all this crap. I'm starting to change my opinion of you."

I wanted to tell him that I'd give reason after reason not to in the months to come, but of course I couldn't. I could only show him, and I would.

Creech cornered me in the back of the warehouse an hour before work ended.

"That Trinitron box you gave me?" He said it quietly, almost gently, so that he didn't sound angry, but I knew what was coming and checked out his hands. They were empty. "That box was full of shit. Busted plates, food, a three-legged stool. That wasn't what we paid for."

I pretended nonchalance even though I was nervous about how this would play out. "I had to. Reemer was suspicious. It was a dry run."

"Don't give me that crap." His voice was curt without being loud. He didn't have to be. He had my full attention. "I'm not a moron. We want our money back."

I shrugged and tried another tack. "Consider it a Christmas bonus."

"It's July, asshole."

"Christmas came early this year."

He shoved me against the wall; the skin on my shoulder blades scraped against the cinder blocks.

"Don't fuck with us."

"Don't fuck with me." I shoved him back, a surge of adrenaline making me push him farther than I'd intended, but that worked in my favor. He hadn't been expecting it, and now there was too great a distance between us for him to swing and hit me. If he wanted to go, I'd know he was coming. "One of you touches me and you'll never get a full box. Remember, you're talking a few thousand a year. What's the possible loss of a couple hundred dollars each?"

He couldn't think of a quick enough answer before I walked away. When he didn't hit me as I passed, I knew he wasn't going to, ever. He'd wait and wait, hoping I'd come around, so he and Gortney could turn me in. He'd live for that moment until it came. I didn't bother telling him that he might as well give it up now.

Willie? There was no way I could scam him. He didn't care about anything enough to lose money on it. But that was all right because it meant once he got his money—much of which had never been mine—he'd forget I ever existed.

I had an hour before quitting time, so I began shifting pallets into the bay, box after box, their fine dusty smell coating my clothes.

N AILS

Nails are death's little emissaries, dead skin appendages at our bodies' edges, like footholds of what is to come—the Normandy Beaches of time—and yet hardly a better indicator exists of the life within, their color, shape, and markings all unmistakable clues to a person's health. Blue nails? Poorly oxygenated blood. Spooned nails? Iron deficiency or diabetes. Transverse pale bands on the nail surface? Kidney failure or arsenic poisoning.

I click the Dictaphone off when my nurse knocks on the door.

"Mr. Tyler's up next," she says, laying his folder on the filing cabinet.

Beyond the cabinet I see the first brown leaves of the season tick against my window and swirl away, and patches of blue sky alternating with dark clouds. I can't tell if it's going to clear or start to rain.

"Is he here yet?" I ask.

"No. He's not scheduled for half an hour."

Half an hour should be enough time to finish my talk. The nurse leaves after I thank her, and I sort through my yellowed notes, remembering a night in my kitchen years ago. My son, Jamie, stood before me, drunk. I was drunk, too, though compared to him I seemed sober. One A.M. and the house was quiet, my wife, Lisa, asleep upstairs, the only sound the slight hissing of water beginning to roil in the teakettle. On the counter were dishes I'd meant to get to and a note from Lisa, red ink on legal paper, three-inch letters: "TALK TO HIM!" Jamie had driven home drunk three times in a month.

Lisa was right; that wasn't youthful indiscretion. I'd gotten home first and put the water on, and Jamie pulled in soon after. Now we stood grinning at each other from across the room. We'd both been watching the World Series, I at a party and he at The Nines, his favorite bar.

"Good crowd?" I asked.

"I'm a celebrity there," he said, holding up his spread fingers. Even in my state I could smell the beer on him, so strong he seemed to have rolled in it. "After nine beers, one for each fingernail, they give me the tenth one free."

When he told me that, I should have made him stop, made him see the danger, but I had driven home drunk, too, even if it was for the first time, and I'd never seen him so happy, almost proud about the nail. Besides, I was always glad to find the spirit of revolt in him, worried that the accident might have left him scared, so I decided not to say anything. Throughout his life I had chosen others over Jamie and

this time I didn't want to do that. How could we talk if I lec-
tured him?

"Here," I said instead, taking his right hand in mine. "Let
me see your nails."

I fumbled with his fingers at first, but finally got a good
grip. The nails were healthy and pink, with white, clearly
marked lunulae, the half moons at the nails' base. All there
of course, except on the middle finger. I'd sliced that nail
off years before. I was a resident, twenty-six, exhausted
from three days on duty with no more than an hour's rest at
a time, reading an article in *The New England Journal of Med-
icine* as I walked upstairs to shower. Jamie followed, chant-
ing my name, my stethoscope dangling from his neck. It
cracked against each stair. I paused at the top of the stairs,
transfixed by some graph or chart, then slammed the door
on Jamie's hand. Lisa said his blond hair stood straight out,
as if he'd been electrocuted—that's what she remembers. I
remember his scream.

Holding his hand, running my finger over the smooth,
shiny bed of the absent nail, I apologized again for the accident.

"Don't worry about it, Dad." He leaned so far back he
knocked the door against the wall and I had to pull him up-
right by his arm. "You did worse things than that."

"Like what?"

When he didn't answer I repeated my question.

"What what?" he said, blinking at me. Then he burped.

"What did I do worse?"

He made an effort to hold his head still. "Nothing. Forget it." He waved his free hand dismissively. "I can't even re-

member if it hurt, and anyway, it's a great conversation starter. That's how I met Carol."

"Nails are pretty interesting, you know," I said. I didn't let go of his hand. It was warm in mine, and small, and I thought again of how he had inherited his mother's build. "It takes about four months for the base of the nail to migrate out to the outer edge, longer as you get older."

"Four months, huh?" His eyes turned glassier. He didn't seem interested, and I wanted him to be, wanted him to see how the accident had come to shape my career, how much his life was caught up in my own, and mine in his. I was afraid I had never communicated that very well, and I didn't think I was doing a good job now. I remember the door frame behind him appearing to wobble, and the floor trying to rise toward me. I wondered how my words sounded.

We seemed like a happy family: a doctor, a corporate planner, a college-age son. But once, standing in the darkened hallway as friends dropped him off, I had heard Jamie say he hated me, something I had said years before about my own father. Though I knew I had done little to make Jamie feel otherwise, I wanted to, I had always wanted to. This was my chance, so I talked on. I told him about what I'd learned, mentioning Mees lines, transverse pale lines on the nail surface, which sometimes indicate arsenic poisoning, and after a while Jamie laughed. "You should write a book about this stuff, Dad."

His voice had an edge and I couldn't tell if he'd meant it as an insult or a compliment. I took his other hand, too, deciding it was the latter. I wanted it to be, and he'd never been nasty to me, and now that his words were slurred with liquor

I'd probably just misinterpreted the tone. Still, I must have looked hurt.

"Really," he said. "I've never seen you this excited about anything."

He probably hadn't, but he didn't know the real reasons for my excitement. He stared at his hands in mine but made no move to pull away and I was glad. This was the first time I'd held his hands in maybe fifteen years, since he used to walk on my feet, dancing around the living room on those rare nights when I came home early and not overburdened with work, when I could take the time to play with him, time I always loved.

The teakettle started its shrill whistling, the jet of steam blotting out our reflection in the mirror behind the sink.

"Want some tea?"

"Tea? Fuck no. What would I want tea for? I don't need more liquid. My stomach sloshes when I walk."

"That's you? I thought maybe it was me."

Finally he took his hands away and put them first in his front pockets, then his back. Then he pulled them out and inspected the nails, holding them away from him the way women do instead of turned inward like men. Then he closed his eyes, shutting them for so long I thought maybe he'd passed out on his feet.

The kettle was still whistling, and before Lisa heard it and came down and found us both wobbling around I went to shut it off.

"Arsenic," he said when I did, and opened his eyes. He seemed not to notice that any time had passed. He was leaning back against the wall, and suddenly he slid to the floor, cracking his chin on one of his knees. He splayed his fingers on the linoleum for balance. A trickle of blood appeared from the corner of his mouth; he'd probably bitten his tongue. "Nope. Doesn't look like Carol's tried that one on me yet."

"Give her time," I said, and laughed. He laughed, too. Blood dripped onto the floor.

That night has never left me. I helped him up and cleaned his face and he went off to bed, both of us knowing that the night was over. He'd been drunk, but that didn't matter. We'd talked. I was sad that more of our lives couldn't be like that and yet I believed they could be. The glory of change filled me, made me dream of what our lives would be like. All the difficulties we'd had during his adolescence, the fights, the silent fuming afternoons and evenings—repeats of the fights I'd had with my own father—all those problems seemed about to fall away like a shell. I remembered Jamie as a newborn. I stood above his crib, watching him suck on the skin between his thumb and forefinger as he slept, and swore I would never be like my father. I had failed, but I could change. I would change.

I was so excited I couldn't sleep. I started taking notes toward a book, as he'd suggested. I knew he probably wouldn't remember, but I'd write it as a surprise for him, to explain to him how our lives were connected. Twice I stopped to check that he hadn't vomited in his sleep, the second time rolling him onto his side, pulling the sheet up to his shoulders, wiping the last blood from his cheek.

I never finished the book. Jamie died two months later. The undertaker attached a fake nail to his finger, believing the real one lost in the crash. I asked him to take it off. He demurred and I insisted. I wanted Jamie to look the way he really had, wanted the mark I'd made on him left visible.

Nails protect the sensitivity of the tips of the fingers and toes, and are used for offensive and defensive activities. In the hands, the nails increase the fine function of the fingertips. They grow at a remarkably constant rate throughout one's life, though that rate varies considerably between people. It takes about four months for the base of the nail to migrate out to the outer edge, a bit longer as we age. The nails on the dominant hand grow faster, as do the nails on longer fingers. Men's nails grow more quickly than women's, but pregnant women's grow quickest of all. Acute illness causes nail growth to stop altogether, leaving discernible bands across all the nails on one or both hands, which can tell a physician how long ago, for instance, someone suffered a serious febrile illness. Make sure the markings occur on all nails of at least one hand; otherwise, they indicate merely local trauma.

I stop again, remembering the trooper pulling into our driveway, his boots squeaking over the snow in the bitter cold. I'd been waiting up for Jamie, hoping we could talk again. I knew before the trooper got out of the car what he was there to tell me, and I realized that I had known on some level that this moment might come, that I was in many ways to blame for it. I crouched and refused to open the door, as if that might somehow change his news. I felt suddenly thrust outside time. Jamie liked tea. His favorite color was teal blue. In ninth grade he took two silver dollars from my dresser and returned them a week later. I knew because the dates on the new ones were wrong. The old ones had been 1958 and 1969—the first the year of Jamie's birth; the second, of my father's death. I often looked at them, and on the anniversaries of those events had carried both with me as reminders, the coins clinking in my pocket. Jamie did not know it, but I had been watching him, all the time.

Wind buffeted the windows and the trooper knocked again and I stood up and opened the door. I called upstairs for Lisa. I don't remember her coming downstairs or what the trooper said or even what he looked like, but I do remember finding, for weeks after the funeral, on windowsills and bookcases and once in a bureau drawer, open-faced triangular sandwiches someone had made and which guests had bitten into and put aside. The bread was stiff, the egg salad and tuna white and blue with mold. And I remember fat George Stevens' arrival first thing the morning after we heard. Goodyear George, we called him, after the blimp. He was the fattest doctor in the city, so big he looked like he went home and injected himself with cortisone each day. He loomed in our doorway, snow blowing behind him, clutching a picture of flowers. No florists were open yet, and the picture was all he could find. I still have it on my desk: pink tulips bursting through snow.

I remember the fight with the undertaker but very little from the funeral itself. At the end I was standing by the casket, oppressed by the smell of flowers. I shook over two hundred hands as people filed by. One of Jamie's friends, obviously nervous, took my hand and said, "I'm sure glad to be here!" and then, mortified, burst into tears. His father hugged him and led him away.

Because of a trauma to my son's nail when he was very young I read a lot about nails. The first diagnosis I ever made strictly on the basis of nails was of a bum in Boston City's emergency room, delirious and screaming. He had methyl alcohol poisoning. His orange nails waved above him as he screamed; he'd squeezed the alcohol from Sterno and drunk it. It destroyed his retinal tissue, blinding him, and then—a nephrotoxin—his kidneys. We could do little except shoot him full of morphine so his death was less painful.

The Dictaphone's battery light blinks, and I sort through my drawers for new ones. The old ones clatter in the wastebasket and I sit for a minute, enjoying the suspension of thought, but before long the picture of the screaming bum leaks back into my mind. Watching that intense physical pain created a bond between me and patients that has lasted to this day: I don't like to see them suffer, physically or emotionally, and I have done everything in my power since to keep them from having to. At times that has caused strains in my marriage—working late when I should have been home for anniversaries or birthdays or spending time with Jamie, going on house calls in the middle of the night and leaving my wife to wake up alone.

It has also meant I've made a lot of money. We took family trips each winter, and I sent Jamie to soccer camp every summer for ten years, on a trip to France with his French club in eleventh grade. Didn't those count for something, in some way make up for the absences that my work demanded?

That I had to ask told me—even then—that it probably
didn't, but I couldn't watch that kind of pain, still can't, and
trying to relieve it is easier than the emotional mess of personal relationships. A kind of escapism, I know, but one I was
willing to embrace—all the more, I'm sure, because of the
profound gratitude people expressed when I helped them: I
was a doctor, the next best thing to God, holding their fate
in my hands. So I kept seeing more and more patients, di-
agnosing them, curing some, losing others, receiving their
thanks. I have a shoebox full of their letters. At home I was
just a husband and a father. Often, I think, a poor one.

For years that bond I felt with patients also made me lose
respect for surgeons. Most seemed more concerned with
money than with their patients, whom they treated with less
care than a good butcher does his meat. But I wonder now
if beneath that indifferent shell, in the walled precincts of
their hearts, many don't hold more suffering than we can
possibly know. George Stevens was like that. He never
talked to his patients in the hospital before surgery, not even
to calm them while drawing directional lines on their skin
with purple dye; he said it distracted him. And after opera-
tions he gave them only cursory attention, checking to be
sure they weren't in unusual pain. Patients often complained.
I used to say he had more contact with them through the mail
than he did in person, and I didn't like that he used his high
fees to buy a Rolls-Royce.

Even so, nobody deserves what befell him—returning
from a vacation and finding his son dead, a suicide, in the
garage. The boy had turned on the Rolls and asphyxiated
himself. This was years before my own boy died, and though

I didn't know George well and didn't particularly like him, I felt someone should be with him. He was divorced, and his wife had moved away, and so, after the funeral, I went to his house every night for two weeks and made him come out for supper. He never said a word during any of the meals. I had to order for him without knowing what he liked. It didn't matter. He ate everything. After dinner the last night, as we pulled into his driveway, he said, "Not tonight." He started wagging his big head and I thought he was going to cry. "I just can't go in there alone."

So we went to bars. He could drink even more than he could eat, and after a couple of hours I stopped trying to keep up with him. Toward the end of the night he asked if I'd ever met his wife. I hadn't and told him so. I realized that she hadn't been at the funeral.

"You would have liked her," he said, fishing a cherry from the bottom of his manhattan and sucking it from its stem. "Everybody did." The music in the bar was too loud and I had to lean close to hear him. Once or twice his lips brushed against my ear, wet with liquor, which made a chill run up and down my spine. It seemed too intimate; despite all the time we'd spent together recently I didn't know him at all. Still, I couldn't pull away from him, not as he was about to open up. So I made myself listen.

"She was pretty, beautiful even, and very smart, far smarter than me. For a long time I couldn't believe my luck. Then one day, this was when we lived up in Boston where I got my training, we were driving home during rush hour. Traffic was unusually slow, all bunched into one lane. When we got to the Ninety-three underpass we found out why:

someone was standing on the bridge, over the guardrail, looking like he might jump.

"We could see him for a long time—five, ten minutes. Firemen were on the bridge, their truck lights flashing, talking to him, and some others were down below, setting up a net across three lanes. My wife never saw any of this. She was too intent on the jumper. She kept rubbing frost from the windshield to get a clearer view. When we got right under him she said, 'Jump. Jump.' She said it very quietly, almost whispered, and at first I thought I hadn't heard her right, but when I looked at her face I knew I had. She was smiling. She really wanted him to."

George sat back, sighed, downed another drink, then leaned toward me again. He smelled like whisky and peanuts. "I knew right then she wasn't the woman I thought she was when I married her, and that I didn't want to find out who she really was."

In the morning, back at his house, I walked him into the bathroom, steadying him with both hands. It felt like trying to steer a warehouse on wheels. He threw up in the bathtub while I held his shoulders. The only thing that makes me sick is other people getting sick and I could feel the liquor and water in my stomach beginning to slosh like ink in a bottle, so I started to get up from the floor. He gripped my sleeve and refused to let me go. The suit jacket I had on that night is permanently lopsided. Between bouts of vomiting he told me he slept every night in his son's bed, trying to imagine what his life had been like, and what had made him do it. He was resting his cheek against the porcelain tub and looking at me sideways. He raised his head, a red streak pressed into his jowl, and said, "I'd put on his clothes if I could fit into them. I wear his shoes. They're the only things of his I fit into. These are his," he said, lifting one loafered foot. He lay his head down again and the fat settled over the rim. Then he cried.

I called in sick for both of us. All those years George had probably never talked to his son. No wonder he had driven himself so hard as a doctor.

Over the next months I read more. Soon I diagnosed a patient who had stumped my fellow residents. She presented with pitted nails but no other symptoms. It was a marker of hidden psoriasis, signs of which are most easily discerned on the thumbnail; checking her elbows and knees confirmed the disease. Then I diagnosed a patient who even my adviser was unable to help. The patient was a middle-aged male who couldn't keep his nails clean. He'd seen four doctors and all told him to wash his hands more frequently. Now his skin was raw from the repeated washings and his nails were still filthy. Plummer's nails, I said on rounds, a sign of Graves' disease, a type of hyperthyroidism. The white of the nail is raised off the underlying tissue and dirt collects in kind of a sawtooth fashion beneath it. The patient had no goiter, and no other obvious symptoms—emaciation, profuse sweating, raised basal metabolism—and the senior doctors, so impressed by what they assumed to be my encyclopedic knowledge of symptoms and signs, appointed me chief resident the next July. It was luck, of course, that allowed me to make that diagnosis, but so began my career, shaped by what had happened in my son's life and not my own.

The intercom buzzes—my receptionist, telling me that Mr. Tyler is late and that Mrs. Williams, my three-thirty, is here early. She wants to know if she should send her in.

"No. I've got a few remarks left to make."

I want to finish my talk in one sitting, before the world of patients draws me away, as it has from so many things— always one of Lisa's chief complaints.

Jamie's death is a quiet space between us even during the best moments, a slight but persistent pull, like water above an open drain spinning beneath your palm. Others don't notice this. Strangers are always surprised when they find out about our boy's death. They say we look too happy for it to be true.

Last year the two of us went on a walking tour of southern Portugal. I hoped the trip would prove a respite from our busy lives, and also that it might restore to us something we'd lost after we lost Jamie. We spent days hiking through wheat fields, with only the wind rattling the wheat, an occasional bird call, our quiet footfalls on the pocket macadam, and our voices, loud in the silence, small against the vastness of the horizon. No cars. Every day the sky was blue, the sun burned, and the air was clear and light, changed only by a sudden heaviness around a water hole or well. We ate lunch in the small towns we passed through, three or four whitewashed buildings dazzling in the sun, blue trim painted around their windows and doors. For luck, we were told. After the first stop, where men had come out to stare at Lisa's bare legs as we sat at a dusty table, we would stop while she pulled on a long linen skirt before walking into town.

At the end of the trip we came to Monsaraz, a whitewashed, fourteenth-century town famous for its tranquillity, and sat high up on its crumbling orange walls to watch the sunset. Birds flocked, chasing clouds of gnats over the broad plains of wheat, and a shepherd drove his sheep up the slopes through the sparse cork oaks toward the walls, his staff tapping at their legs. My legs were comfortably tired; my breathing began to slow. I could smell the wall's crumbling mortar, the faint but pungent odor of sheep dung, the tang of my own drying sweat. Talked out, we sat in silence. In the fading light I could not see the small wrinkles etched around Lisa's eyes or the gray streaking her hair, so it was almost as if she were young again but for the shadow that played across her features and that no doubt crossed mine as well.

Sounds grew more distinct in the dark, as if the absence of light gave them weight and form, and so it was with emotions. Children's laughter rose up from somewhere behind us in the town. It hurt to hear it just then, so much so that the pain felt like a physical reprimand. Lisa, seeming to know my feelings, reached out and took my hand. I listened to the tinny ring of sheep bells for a long time, thinking that what I regretted most were missed opportunities: times I yelled at Jamie and meant to apologize, things I said to him and wanted to explain, or things I never said and should have.

Once, as he and I drove home from my nephew's funeral, I said, "Your mother and I would be devastated if anything happened to you." That was the closest I ever came to saying I loved him, but even then, instead of looking at him, I was watching the windshield wipers and shifting gears. A few years later, while we were deep in the woods cutting down a Christmas tree, I said that Mark, an older boy we both knew, the son of a friend of mine and always in trouble, would do his parents a favor if he showed up dead. I wondered how I could think such a thing, let alone say it, and which of those two comments my own son might have remembered.

I wanted to talk to Lisa about this, hoping that she could reassure me, and I even said her name, but she pressed my arm in the growing dark, a sign that she wanted me not to talk. Those first weeks after his death she would cover her mouth and wave me away whenever I brought up Jamie's death, and feeling that I was making it harder on her I waited. Her reaction has never changed. Even now when I call her Charlotte—I never use her real name except when I'm serious—she shakes her head, her eyes instantly welling, and, her hands out as if to keep me at bay, says, "I can't. I just can't." So I keep my silence. For years I had the chance to talk and didn't; now, when I want to, I can't. I see it as a kind of penance.

The first thing a physician should observe is color. Pale nails probably indicate anemia, which in women usually means iron deficiency, in men, colon cancer. Women get that way from too much menstrual flow, eating clay, or eating only starch, real starch, from the box. When I was younger I came across a lot of black women who got their entire caloric intake that way, and it has no iron. Either way, iron deficiency often causes an unusual craving for ice, so the physician should always ask if patients have been eating ice when she sees pale nails. A single brown longitudinal line always indicates Addison's disease—adrenal hypofunction. Yellow nails indicate a fungal infection or lymphatic abnormalities, blue, poor oxygenation. But doctors must pay attention to the temperature when nails are blue. Blue and cold hands means poor circulation. Blue and warm indicates the blood isn't picking up oxygen in the lungs, and therefore something is wrong with the lungs—an infection, perhaps, or maybe cancer. If the nail is overtly red it indicates superoxygenation, the result of too much blood. Polycythemia. To treat it, we draw off blood at regular intervals.

If the lunula is azure blue, the patient has Wilson's disease— excess copper accumulation—a disease so rare that it's not listed in most medical dictionaries, and complete absence of the lunula indicates either kidney or liver failure, the latter usually from al- coholism. Lines under the nails are important, too. Red ones, called splinter hemorrhages, indicate heart disease or vasculitis, and in black men are a sure sign of sickle-cell anemia. At the prox- imal base of the nail, along the nail fold, the lines usually mean lupus. Transverse pale bands, called Mees lines, show cyclic peri- ods of poor protein nutrition, which again usually mean kidney problems, or indicate that someone's been poisoned with arsenic. There will be a noticeable band across the whole nail for each at- tempt at murder.

The day after he died I remembered having talked with Jamie about those lines. I was thinking about him constantly, of course, and about how there are those who leave before they are gone—I see it often, a patient in whom something breaks or gives up or dies and before long the rest of her fol- lows. And then there are those who go before they are ready. Jamie was like that, not yet fully formed, casting about in his college courses for something to latch on to. He had told me once only that he knew he was going to be anything but a doctor. I understood that. I had told my father I would be anything but a lawyer. Still, I enjoyed watching Jamie search.

Not the struggle, of course, but the expectancy, the waiting to see what he would become.

I couldn't get past that, how he was never going to get the chance to find what it was in life he truly liked or hated. I lay motionless on my living room couch day after day, listening to my own breathing and drifting in and out of sleep, able to tell the difference between the two states only from a coppery taste in my mouth, or sat in a closet with books, turning their pages without reading them, or went out back and threw stones at trees until my arm was too sore to lift. Then George Stevens showed up at our door and asked if I wanted to take a ride.

Once we were out, driving around the city, I became aware of his labored breathing, the way air seemed to come a long way in order to escape his lungs. It was as if he had to think about breathing, to remind himself to do it. I wondered if that's how I sounded now, too.

After a few miles, he said, "You need to see patients again."

"Did that help you?"

"Nothing helps. But you can forget for a while, concentrating on something else."

He was right, of course, and I went back to work. Soon my breathing stopped sounding like George's and I was surprised at how the sharp sting of loss eventually dulled, flaring only at odd moments: seeing a boy who ran like Jamie once in a park, or seeing another who looked like I had as a teenager. His face, as yet unmarked by knowledge of real pain, reminded me of all that I'd experienced in the decades that separated us, things I hoped he would never have to. And yet, nineteen seems younger each year, so now it is as if Jamie died a child.

By this time I had acquired a widespread knowledge of the various diseases associated with nail deformities, and other doctors were referring their patients to me if their patients presented with nail abnormalities. This had a kind of exponential effect: the more subjects I saw with odd nails and the more I read about the diseases that might cause these oddities, the easier it became for me to diagnose patients' problems. I learned that longitudinal canals on the surface of nails usually mean nutritional deficiencies—vitamins C and B_2, calcium or magnesium—and are often associated with eating disorders; that beading almost always reveals thyrotoxicosis, that Raynaud's disease, a vascular problem chiefly affecting women, is revealed in nails years before other signs appear.

During one extraordinary week I diagnosed three different patients just from looking at their nails. The first was a Southern woman who had moved north recently; she came in with spooned nails and crescents of purple clay beneath them. The spooning—koilonychia—was not quite evident to the naked eye, but I dripped water onto her thumbnail and it stayed beaded up instead of rolling off, an excellent diagnostic clue. And since the nails were thin the spooning meant anemia; thickened spooned nails indicates diabetes. She was pregnant, I told her, and anemic; the clay she ate deprived her body of iron. I knew she was pregnant and eating clay even without her telling me. That was common then among rural women from the deep South, though less so now—a folk cure for constipation. Next was a man whose fingers and nails were clubbed, painful to the touch, and nicotine-stained, which meant he probably had lung cancer. X rays confirmed an inoperable bronchogenic cancer of the lung; it killed him in less than a year. Two days later I saw a girl whose nails, palms, tongue, and eyelids were bright red, as if she'd dipped them in paint. She had leukemia. Fortunately, we caught it early enough to cure.

I am still learning what nails can reveal. Recently, I have found that ringworm on the nails is common in HIV patients, more common on the feet than the hands. Nails become lusterless, brittle, and hypertrophic, the infection usually spreading from the distal edges inward. It can be one of the earliest indicators of the disease. Unfortunately, the medication for ringworm, griseofulvin, has powerful side effects, and the physician is obligated to explain to patients they risk worsening their general health by taking it. Careful explanation of long-term effects of any treatment are crucial in building physician-patient trust.

I rewind the tape and listen to what I have already said. After my voice stops, I hear the tape clicking, and then a steady, quiet hiss. As much as I mean them, the words convey only a portion of my feelings. Somehow, the silence seems to do that better.

I hope the talk is not too dry, but as my audience is young medical students who are still fascinated by the body's minutiae and who see the body as a thing to be studied, poked, pried into, mastered, instead of a set of signposts to a more ephemeral being, it probably won't be. They have yet to learn that the people they treat will mark them, too.

We talk abstractly as doctors, denying any emotional attachment to our subjects. Being scientific, we say. I think it more likely we seek to spare ourselves.

So this is a brief summary of some of the clues to health that nails can give. I hope all of you, at some point in your careers, will investigate the many others.

I would like to dedicate this talk to my son, Jamie, whose small hands were the source of my initial interest in nails and whose grown ones taught me the value of patience. Even now, holding others' hands in mine, I am reminded always of the touch of his.

I back that section up and listen twice to myself speaking my son's name, and to what I say about him. All true, but my son is of little interest to other doctors, I imagine, and even less their business, so I erase it.

I have learned, through the study of nails, the value of listening to people, of taking time with them. One discovers more from looking and listening to what a patient has to say about his or her own body than from all the high-powered tests we order routinely. I urge you to think carefully about changing the way you use them. It is not that those tests don't have their purpose—they do—but it is the combination of close scrutiny of what often appear to be the most minor physical details and the words people speak that can tell us most clearly which tests to use and why.

Change can come too late, even for the living. When my own father reached out to me in the end I turned away, too angry from the years of silence. But I am glad now that I outlived him, that he was spared the pain of burying his son. It never disappears.

George died young. Fat men usually do. Sometimes we would have lunch together at the hospital cafeteria in the years after our sons' deaths. I no longer remember what we talked about, though I do remember long silences when I knew we were both thinking of the same things, and I remember watching him eat, still amazed by his appetite and aware that we both knew he was digging his own grave with his teeth, as my father used to say of fat men. I never brought that up. I was sure many others did, and George appeared grateful for my silence. In some ways his experiences didn't change him much, and yet he comforted me in my time of greatest sorrow, something he might not have done had he not experienced similar pain. I don't think that's uncommon. The changes we look for in others after traumatic events frequently emerge as mere shadows. I hope my own change has been more profound, but I have come to realize that a vast gulf often lies between that which we hope for and that which others perceive.

The nurse knocks, sticks her head in the door.

"Mr. Tyler is finally ready," she says, tapping his chart with her nails to remind me.

I nod, my head down, put aside the talk, pick up his file—which I still haven't read—and go in to greet him. He is sitting in full sunlight on the examining table, a large, heavy black man with sagging shoulders and dulled eyes, probable signs of mild depression, perhaps induced by pain.

He is still dressed, as I requested—a request that surprises patients the first time they see me.

I introduce myself, shake his hand, don't let go. His fingers are broadened and flattened and callused by years of work. I ask him how his drive in was, if he had to wait long to see me, if he's going to watch the game tonight. His replies, unenthusiastic, directed at the wall over my shoulder instead of to me, strengthen my initial suspicion of depression. With my left hand I palpate his flexed wrist, with my right I hold his fingertips up to the sunlight to determine their warmth, color, circulation. The nail beds have some paint stains on the cuticle and the nail folds—indicating that he's let down on his care over the last few months—and on the thumbnail the thickened leading edge has begun to pull away from the underlying skin, mild onycholysis.

"You're a painter?" I ask, pressing his thumbnail, trying to rock it.

"Now the secretary already asked me all that. It's in my chart."

"I haven't read it yet," I say.

"Then how come I had to fill it all out?" He pulls his hand free, which I don't resist. Patients must trust you before they'll say anything important, and building that rapport is a kind of seduction. I have to let him move comfortably, even if for a while that means moving away.

"Oh, insurance companies like them." I smile to reassure him, my own hands folded in front of me. "But I like to find things out by talking to patients, especially on the first visit. After all, you usually know what's wrong."

I listen to the air being forced into the room through the air-conditioning duct while he looks me over, trying to decide, I imagine, if I'm serious. Sunlight and shadows play over his shoulders as the wind stirs the branches outside the window.

"Well, all right then," he says, finally. He extends his hand, slowly, giving me another chance, and I take it again. "Yes sir, I am a painter."

"And you open a lot of cans with a screwdriver and this thumbnail?"

"Um-hmm," he says, interested now, watching my fingers move over his own.

More important than the staining are the splinter hemorrhages beneath the nails, dark red lines like scores of slivers worked under the skin, and the poor manicure, a further sign of depression. His pain has obviously worn him down.

"Have you had any abdominal pain recently?" I ask.

"Terrible. Hurts like hell. Can't even sleep on my stomach anymore."

"Any sores on your ankles?"

"A bunch." He shifts his legs on the seat, as if even discussing them makes them hurt.

"You've got sickle-cell anemia," I say, and I know I'm right. I squeeze his hand once before letting it go, then write down a few notes on the outside of his file.

"How do you know that? Don't you have to run some tests?"

"Just to prove it, yes. But it's the nails. They're a sure sign."

I take up his hands once more, which already feel familiar in my own. I am going to talk to him, show him the lines, tell him what they mean, how they reveal his history and foretell parts of his future, and then discuss treatments, the ways in which his life might change. And so I begin again, palm to fingertips, fingertips to palm.

WHY SHOULD I WAIT?

————————————

In June, Bolen blew into a small town just south of Cleveland without a cent to his name and talked himself onto a construction job at a hospital, working on the structural steel for an addition. One of the Navajo ironworkers had gone up drunk and come down hard just before Bolen arrived, and Bolen found the foreman in a blue safety hat, looking over the dusty pit where the new building's skeleton was rising. His name was Robinson. Bolen had to tug on his sleeve to get his attention over the clanking of cranes lifting steel into place.

"He had enough sense to fall on the inside," Robinson said, pointing out parts of the building with a copy of the blueprints rolled up in his hand. He was the only black man Bolen had ever seen with green eyes, and at first it disconcerted him. "But he was still busted up pretty bad. Both arms broke and his left knee twisted around backward. Two of his friends quit on the spot."

"Bad karma?" Bolen said, joking. He spit to get rid of the diesel taste from the cranes' smoke. It had been a couple of years since he'd been around it steadily, and he'd forgotten how it coated the roof of his mouth like oil.

"No, no. That's the other type of Indians. You know, from overseas. They don't go up on high-rises."

Bolen let it go. It was just another case of him being smarter than everyone he'd have to work with if he got the job, but he didn't care. He pressed a bottle cap into the dirt with the heel of his boot and covered it over.

Robinson was also the general contractor, and this was his first big job. Things were going poorly for him: workers getting hurt, materials either not delivered or disappearing from the site, lousy weather. He rubbed his hand back and forth over his stubbly hair, sighing at his bad luck, and asked Bolen if he was afraid of heights.

"No."

"Do you drink?"

"Not while I'm working."

"Have you ever worked with structural steel before?"

"Oh yeah." He looked Robinson in the eye. He'd put a beam in a house once, but he doubted that's what Robinson meant. Still, it was worth a shot. He needed the money. And he was tired of sleeping in his car and taking day jobs. He wanted to stay someplace long enough to call it home.

Robinson tapped the blueprints against his thigh, studying Bolen, then turned back to the steel skeleton and watched the crane lower a bundle of plywood into place. The job was

already a month and a half behind schedule, and he decided
then and there that he would use any bodies that showed up.
He just didn't have the time to go looking for them.

"Two out of three isn't bad," he said.

Bolen laughed. "Which one don't you believe?"

"Now, we'll just find out, won't we?"

Bolen learned how to shoot bolts and to direct the cranes so
they'd set the load in their slings right, even how to weld,
and he liked it. But a month into the job heavy rains came
and Bolen spent three days with nothing to do. Each morning he'd report to one of the trailers at six-thirty, eat some
doughnuts and drink a few cups of coffee while pacing the
muddy floor, and spend the day checking the windows every
five minutes to see if the rain had let up. Finally, going crazy
without work, he asked Robinson to put him on another de-
tail—anything, just so he wasn't sitting around.

"Ever work with marble saddles?" Robinson said, pushing a box of doughnuts to a corner of the plans.

"Once or twice."

"Think you can put them in without ruining them?"

"Sure." Bolen was never one to volunteer the possibility
of his own shortcomings.

The saddles were delicate work. They covered the flooring gaps between rooms in a part of the old hospital being
renovated, and they had to be broken at just the right places
or the marble would fracture along veins in the stone. With
wood or metal that didn't matter, but marble was too expensive to waste. Bolen got the work because the mason already on the job turned out to be a drunk: every morning

when the coffee truck came he pulled a flask of bourbon from his coveralls and laced his coffee. An hour later he'd slip past Robinson, ducking his head. "Going for supplies," he'd say, and head out to his van and fall asleep in the back, face pressed up against a stack of pipes. Once again Robinson didn't want to lose time on hunting up a replacement.

Kenny, one of Robinson's sons, carted the marble from room to room in a wheelbarrow and mixed the saddle mortar in a plastic bucket he dragged along the floor behind him. He had knotty muscles in his forearms, and knees that bowed outward. When Bolen didn't need him, he'd find a corner and take a few hits from one of the joints he kept in a plastic bag in his shirt pocket. There were eight of them when he arrived each morning and he smoked one an hour.

The first saddle Bolen broke into jagged shards. He flushed, feeling Kenny watching him, and cursed himself silently. He bent over the pieces a long time, trying to remember how he'd done the work before, all the while conscious of Kenny's presence. He wondered if Robinson had sent him to spy. With his heavy eyelids and high top fade he always looked like he'd just gotten out of bed, but Bolen suspected he was watching closely.

Once, holding his own breath while he tried notching the saddle with a hacksaw, he heard a long, slow letting-go of breath from Kenny and whipped around, expecting to see him pointing to his watch. He wasn't. He'd fired up a joint. He raised his eyebrows quizzically and held it out, grinning.

Bolen turned him down and went back to work, practicing with the shards, trying to find a way that would break them cleanly. Finally, after half an hour or so, he remem-

bered tiling a bathroom, how he scored the short tiles before snapping off their edges. He tried it and stood smiling
over the results. Perfect. After that the work went smoothly.

The rooms were all dark and faintly cool and dusty, with
half-finished walls and loose wires hanging from jagged holes
in the Sheetrock. Plaster dust coated the black linoleum
floors like flour; footprints tracked across them. Bolen liked
the challenge of the marble, tracing veins with his fingernail
to see where they could be broken cleanly, and he liked the
heavy, cool feel of the saddles in his hands.

By eleven-thirty he'd put in more than half, and stopped
briefly to check the plans. Some doorways were supposed
to get metal or wood saddles, mostly those out of sight or
within offices. The one he stopped at was a bathroom, and
he'd just told Kenny to trowel out the mortar when something about the plans caught his eye.

"Hold it, Kenny," Bolen said. "Let me figure this out."
Kenny took a seat in the bathtub and lighted a joint. Now
and then he stirred the mortar with his trowel, to keep it
from stiffening prematurely.

Bolen brought the plans to the window, sneezing from the
dust, and studied them in the light. This was a handicapped
bathroom, with an extra-wide doorway and handrails bolted
into the wall beside the toilet and bath. The raised saddle
would be hard for people in wheelchairs to get over.

The weather had finally cleared. Outside he could see the
architect, standing by a black Mercedes, checking some papers
spread across the hood. He was wearing a blue-and-white-
striped shirt that Bolen guessed must have cost seventy-five
dollars. He couldn't have been much older than Bolen.

"I bet it's leased," Bolen said to Kenny, about the car. Kenny had his feet up on an overturned plastic bucket, and his eyes were bloodshot. He had no idea what Bolen was talking about.

"Here," he said, careful not to let any smoke escape when he spoke. "Have a hit." He held the joint out to Bolen.

"No—I don't want any of that shit," Bolen said.

He watched a blond woman drive up in a white Toronado and park behind the Mercedes. She fixed her lipstick in the mirror, then got out and shook the architect's hand. She was carrying a leather briefcase. Bolen had seen her before. She was the banker in charge of construction loans and she came out to the job once or twice a week to inspect the progress. Bolen liked the way her silver bracelet flashed in the sunlight when she pointed to things, and how nice her calves were beneath her dress as she went up the dusty stairs in the building.

He could see the strong curve of her back as she bent over to look at the papers with the architect. Bolen figured this was a good chance to impress them both. He scrubbed his hands and face and checked his reflection in a dusty mirror, rubbing a spot clean with his forearm. He put some water on his fingertips and smoothed down his hair, then grabbed one of the marble saddles and bounded down the stairs.

"Hey, chief," he said to the architect. "I think you got a problem with these saddles." He held it up and smiled at the banker. He could smell her flowery perfume. A long strand of her hair had fallen onto her dress and he had to restrain himself from brushing it away.

"They fit, don't they?" the architect said.

"Sure."

"Then there's no problem."

"I think there is. I mean, unless you want speed bumps for the wheelchairs." He dropped the saddle on the roof of the car and pushed his fingers against it to demonstrate what he meant. "You ought to go with something else, something flatter in the handicapped bathrooms."

The architect didn't get the joke, and Bolen could tell he didn't like being second-guessed in front of the banker—his fake smile was gone, and he stood to his full height, a few inches taller than Bolen. He took the saddle from his roof, handed it to Bolen, then checked the finish for scratches, rubbing his fingers over it as if it were some kind of fine fabric.

The banker shooed a fly from the plans. She didn't even glance at Bolen.

"We'll look into it," the architect said, nodding dismissively. Bolen knew he wouldn't. The architect bent over the plans again, briefly putting his hand on the banker's back. "Sorry we were interrupted."

When Bolen went back he told Kenny to break for lunch, then troweled enough mortar into the flooring gap to fill it level. He lay the saddle on the mortar, tamped it in place with the butt of the trowel, and stepped on it to be sure it was anchored. The mortar oozed out over the floor.

After waiting for the saddle to set, Bolen spread a layer of mortar over it, put another saddle on top, then stood on the two of them for a couple of minutes. He repeated the process twice more. Then he made a sign out of a cardboard box, SECURITY CHECKPOINT FOR WHEELCHAIRS, and cemented it beneath the last saddle. There was enough mortar that the

saddles would have to be taken out with jackhammers. Satisfied, he walked off the job for the rest of the day.

The next morning, when Bolen showed up for work, Robinson pulled him into his trailer. A Mr. Coffee pot bubbled on
a small wooden table by the door and its aroma filled the
room. Robinson took a seat behind his desk, lips pursed, staring out the window. On his arms, veins bulged just under
the skin, thick as fingers. A brass alarm clock ticked quietly,
and Bolen realized Robinson was going to let him wait, so
he looked around. It was the neatest trailer he'd ever seen
on a construction job—papers stacked in three separate piles
on the desk or put away in one of the rows of gleaming metal
file cabinets, linoleum floor swept and polished, even the
windows sparkling in the early sun.

Outside the window Kenny was smashing his pickup into
a tree. He'd bent his bumper out of shape the day before
pulling a load of steel with a cable, and now he was trying
to straighten it by whacking into the tree. He backed up
twenty feet, floored it, hit the tree, and backed up again.
He'd knocked the bark off the tree and the wood underneath
shone pink like salmon. The impact of the collisions shook
the trailer, but Bolen couldn't hear any sound; it was lost in
the general clatter of the job. Robinson shook his head.

"Look, Bolen," he finally said, wheeling around in his
chair to face him. "I covered your ass yesterday, but if you
pull another stunt like that you're gone. Got it?" His green
eyes riveted Bolen.

Bolen was pouring himself a cup of coffee. He held the
steaming pot toward Robinson and asked if he wanted any.

"No, I don't want any coffee. I want to know if you heard me."

A few drops of water dripped from the filter onto the hot plate. Bolen watched them sizzle and dance across it.

"Sure. I heard you." He drank half his cup in one shot.

"Then do something about it. You're a good worker, and I'd like to keep you on. My sons are always so fucked up on one thing or another that I can't trust them to run jobs, and I need someone who's steady. It could be you, but you got to get that temper under control."

Bolen nodded. He'd been thinking that he'd like to keep working for Robinson, too, but he didn't want to let on. Once someone had something you wanted, they'd use it on you. He refilled his cup and put the pot back.

"Well, what do you say?"

Bolen knew the architect had probably told Robinson to fire him, and he'd be madder than hell if he were back on the job. Bolen liked Robinson, and he liked that Robinson had stood up for him.

"All right, boss. Sure. I'm sorry about yesterday. It's just that I was right, and I don't like it when hotshots won't listen to anyone whose butts they don't have to kiss. You don't know how it feels to have assholes like that always underestimate you."

"Look at me."

Bolen did.

"What do you see?"

Bolen shrugged. "I see you, the boss."

Robinson shook his head. "What color am I?"

"You don't need me to tell you that."

"Tell me."

"You're black."

"That's right. I'm black. So don't even begin to tell me I don't know what it's like to be underestimated."

He pointed out the window. "That architect, he's a son of a bitch to you? I'm dealing with a hundred of them every day, and all of them thinking the same damn thing: this guy won't deliver. He's a set-aside. I'm going to take their money and sit my lazy black ass down—that's what they're waiting for. And when this job is done I'm going to shut their faces up and have fun doing it, because I'll be finished here on time. But you being an asshole yourself won't help me do it."

Robinson spread a wax-paper bag of tomato slices on a plate. He sprinkled salt over them, and the moisture on the tomatoes' surface puckered, like a pond struck by raindrops. "I try not to expect much from white folks. That way I'm not disappointed. I didn't expect you to last this long, or to work so hard. Keep it up. And if everything goes according to plan . . ." He looked up at Bolen, the salt shaker poised in his hand, "I'll double your salary."

"Fine." Bolen swallowed the rest of his coffee to hide his surprise and started toward the door, where he rested his hand on the handle. It rattled because his fingers were shaking. Robinson was offering him a lot of money. "Thanks," he said with an effort.

"Thank me by being patient," Robinson said.

Patience wasn't one of Bolen's virtues. When he was a kid, Ralph, his stepfather, yelled at him constantly about how he needed to be more patient if he was ever going to amount to anything. One time, when Ralph was swearing and kicking the car because he couldn't get some nuts off a flat tire, Bolen had said, "Hey, be patient." He thought it was pretty funny, but Ralph hadn't. The ring on his finger tore a hole in Bolen's cheek when he hit him. Bolen still had the dime-size scar.

Bolen's teachers said the same thing about him. One of them had written in his file: "Jeff has an inability to wait for the things he wants."

When he read it, Bolen thought, Why should I wait? And then, tossing it aside, Like this guy knows what I want.

The same teacher wrote, "He lacks the discipline to do assigned tasks."

It wasn't that. He tried as hard as anybody he knew, harder at times, but somehow the information on the pages he read never seemed to sink in. They tracked him with the slow group and that embarrassed him. By high school he'd begun to fight and his stepfather had given up on him. For a year before it happened, Bolen knew they were going to duke it out, and when they finally did he was surprised at how quickly it was over—two punches on his part and Ralph was reeling against the bedroom wall, his mouth bloody, otherwise unhurt, but absolutely stunned.

Bolen lived at a friend's house for a few days, then decided to clear out of town. He broke into the school and stole all of his records, those of other kids he either liked or didn't, and then a few at random, so it would seem like maybe it wasn't him. Scared he'd be found out anyway, he started a fire in the records department.

That line about lacking patience always stuck with him. Once, a question on a job application read: "What is your greatest weakness?"

"I am impatient for success," he wrote. They hired him on the spot, liking the way that sounded. He lasted only a week.

He drifted. At first he didn't mind. He lived in Texas for a year, building swimming pools in working-class neighborhoods during the oil boom, then headed north, finding jobs as a laborer in the baking cornfields of Nebraska in the summer and in the winter as a ski lift operator in Colorado. That's when he first started noticing money, what it meant. Even with a good job—say, working construction and saving half his paycheck each week—he just couldn't figure out how he was going to be rich enough to have a house like the ones on the slopes: soaring wooden places with windows that seemed bigger than his whole town had when he was growing up. They were second homes, and he wondered what these peoples' first ones were like.

For a while he thought it had something to do with school, so when he found the *Harvard Six Foot Shelf of Books* in the trunk of a junked car outside a farm in Kansas, he felt like he'd discovered a treasure map. He'd started reading them right there, sitting in the cramped backseat, beginning with the Greeks. He found them too weird and moved on to Darwin, which was more familiar. He read all afternoon, not minding the wheat chaff under his collar or the flies that bit his sunburned neck when the wind died down, not even minding the growing dark. He didn't stop reading until he couldn't make out the print.

He liked the Shakespeare and a few of the other things, but none of it helped him. No matter how often he read he couldn't absorb much, and what he did didn't seem to make him any smarter. Each page was a struggle, and the effort he put in never felt reflected in what he got back. Still, he swore that someday he was just going to sit down and read the things straight through.

After he put the books aside he started getting tattoos. First an American War Eagle, the top of whose head just stuck out above his T-shirts, attracting people's attention. Soon that wasn't enough, so he kept getting more. He found they made some people scared, which was fine, and others curious. He liked people to notice him one way or the other and he didn't much care what their response was, so long as they had one.

Just before getting this job outside Cleveland, he'd turned thirty. He'd bounced from job to job, picked up tools along the way, learned enough to get by: how to disassemble an engine and how to run a haybine and tedder, how to read blueprints and how to frame a house. But he never felt, This is it. This is how I'm going to make my fortune. He thought he was smarter than most of the foremen he worked under but they were often somebody's brother or husband or son-in-law or friend, and that's how those jobs always went. The rest of the time he got into fights.

But this job seemed different. He worked hard, and Robinson liked him, liked the way he stayed sober and showed up early and worked late without complaining, especially since Robinson had the crew going all hours to get the addition done. Bolen took care to do the job right and

to ask questions about what he didn't know, and he learned
fast. He thought he might at last have caught on somewhere
where he'd have a chance to put aside a good chunk of money
and get ahead.

The crew was the usual mix of ex-cons, drunks, druggies,
and hard workers, and Bolen organized them into stickball
teams during the morning breaks. He sawed off a two-by-
two at thirty-six inches, planed down the corners on the handle to round it, and made balls out of masking tape, joint
compound, and rags. At noon, after everyone ate, they'd
play in the parking lot in front of the Dumpster, in the shade
from the old hospital, hitting balls as far as they could into
the blue sky. He liked that, and the beers after work with
people he didn't know in a new town where everything
seemed possible again, and the rhythm of the work itself:
how during the heat of the day the jokes and conversation
stopped and there was just him alone with the lifting and fitting and welding, his eyes stinging from sweat and the blinding glare of the welding torches, his ears filled with the
sounds of the diesel chuffing of cranes and the clanking of
metal on metal. And he liked how at three-thirty, when the
whistle blew and all the machines shut down at once, it was
suddenly so quiet he thought he'd gone deaf until he heard
the crickets buzzing like crazy, as if to fill up the silence, and
birds calling, and far off the steady background hum of traffic. He also liked the way he could see from day to day the
progress of the building.

But most of all he liked being up on the skeleton in the
early morning. He'd sit straddling one of the beams, looking out over the countryside, and he never thought about

money or the architect or anyone else when he was up there. No matter how hot it got on the ground a breeze almost always cooled his face, and the muffled sounds of church bells and car horns drifted up to him from down below, like he was in another world, just listening to that one. He could see for miles—Cleveland visible over a blue line of hills to the north, spiky in the center, with a few skyscrapers trailing off like a tail, and nearby the houses packed close together with corner grocery stores and gas stations, then the smaller lots giving way to scattered housing tracts, and beyond that just farmhouses and fields of wheat, corn, and oats going right down to the edge of the river in the valley. In the morning the river flashed in the sun and the air up on the skeleton smelled like summer: grass and flowers and warm pavement and dirt and exhaust fumes, and it seemed so alive to him that he often went up early, before anyone else was even on the site, so he'd have a few minutes to himself to breathe it in and to look around and listen.

He picked out houses he'd like to buy if he had the money. There were three of them, two with pools, but it was the one without a pool he finally settled on—a big old white place on top of a hill, with columns and a copper roof, leafy green chestnuts around it for shade, and a pond out back to swim in with cattails at one end, moving in a breeze, and a view over farmland and apple orchards to the river. One Sunday morning he drove out to it. A flock of red-winged blackbirds sat in a field of green oats below the house, stalks bobbing gently from their weight. He guessed there were over a thousand birds. A tractor's engine clattered to life nearby and the flock burst from the oats like a black cloud.

They wheeled, cawing, and a flash of red from two thousand wings shot through the black like a bolt of lightning, and then the birds turned again and the red was gone and they settled into another field.

He drove up into the hills at one end of the valley and watched a storm come toward him. As the clouds got closer small pieces the size of tumbleweeds broke off and spun over the ground, and the green oats twisted wildly in the wind. He turned and raced the storm back to the motel where he rented a room weekly. He went inside and lay on the sagging bed and decided he was going to stick around and get enough money together to buy himself one of those houses.

It didn't work out that way. Not because of his fighting—he didn't get into a fight the whole summer—and not because of run-ins with the architect. He was careful to be polite to the man, even forcing himself to say, "Yes sir," in response to one of his questions. That in itself almost brought trouble, because Bolen could tell by the way the architect glared at him he thought he was being mocked. Bolen couldn't help it—he just didn't carry off humility well. But it was a nurse who eventually forced him to leave.

One morning late in July, when the heat and humidity had been terrible for two weeks straight, he awoke at six o'clock to find heat waves already shimmering on the pavement. By noon he could hardly move: his eyes burned with sweat and he felt like he was trying to breathe water. He decided to eat lunch in the hospital cafeteria for a change and took directions from Robinson without paying much attention. Once

inside, he got lost. After fifteen minutes he found a small
lunchroom off a basement corridor, cool and dark. Walking
into it was like jumping in a pool. He stood in the doorway
looking around and let the cool air wash over his body. These
people had it good.

There weren't any doctors, just nurses and secretaries sitting in groups of three or four at long tables, and they all
looked at him when he entered like he was a walking disease.
His pants were dusty, the pores on his face clogged with dirt,
his hair matted from his hard hat, and his shirt smelled like
sweat. At first he was embarrassed, and after going through
the line and getting his lunch he sat by himself in a corner by
a window, not wanting to offend anyone, but as he thought
about it he got madder and madder. Every now and then one
of the women's heads would pop up from her group like a
chicken's, stare at him, then drop back down. Who the fuck
were they to look at him like that? He could hear them
buzzing as he ate.

He'd paid his money, and he was willing to bet he was
three times as smart as any of them, but what really angered
him was that he knew if he'd shown up wearing a white coat
they would have died to sit next to him. Once at a movie he
overheard a girl from a local college telling a friend that her
mother said she shouldn't bother studying at the regular library. "Go to the law library," she said. "You'll meet somebody who's going to be rich." These women probably
thought the same way.

Finally one came over and stood next to him. He didn't
look up at her, but he could tell by her solid white shoes and
the way she stood, arms straight at her side, hands fisted like

a schoolteacher's over a bad child, that she was probably in charge of some floor. He let her stand there for a while as he ate, and then, after she'd cleared her throat three or four times and he couldn't ignore her any longer, he said, "What do you want?" without looking up at her. He took another bite of his sandwich and was careful not to close his mouth while he chewed.

"Excuse me, sir, but this dining room is for staff only."

"Define staff."

"What?"

"I said, 'Define staff.' You can hear, can't you? You understand English?"

"The staff are people who work here at the hospital." In the window he saw her smile at the top of his head.

"Then I'm staff." Without taking a break from his meal he reached into his back pocket for his wallet, slapped it open on the table, and pulled out his temporary hospital ID with two grimy fingers.

He pointed at the picture on the ID. "Now who's that?"

"You."

"That's right. And damned handsome, if I do say so myself." He put his finger on the signature beside it. "I'll bet you can read, too. Who's that?"

"The director of the hospital."

"Very good. And if he signs my ID, that must mean I work here. And *that* means I'm staff. Now run along and tell your friends to quit talking about me, or tomorrow I'll sit next to them."

"But . . ."

"No buts." He looked at her for the first time, ready to

raise his voice. Her skin was pouchy beneath her eyes—as if she'd been struck—and pinched around her mouth and nose. She looked tired and unhappy, and he realized the heat was probably bothering her, too. Still and all, she shouldn't be insulting him. "Just get lost and let me eat my lunch in peace, okay?"

The next day he came in for lunch wearing a chartreuse T-shirt, so he'd stand out. The more he'd thought about it, the less he was willing to excuse the nurse's behavior. A paper sign on the door said THIS CAFETERIA IS FOR FULL-TIME STAFF ONLY. NO PART-TIME WORKERS, CONSTRUCTION CREW MEMBERS, OR OTHER UNAUTHORIZED PERSONNEL MAY EAT HERE. It was signed by the director of the hospital.

He read the sign twice, thinking about his job and the things he liked—Robinson, the money, the view out over the fields. He'd hate to lose them. Still, none of it was worth letting that witch of a nurse have her way. He conjured up a picture of the house with the copper roof and found it already faded, like a memory.

He spit on his hands, rubbed them together so the dirt on them was damp, and spread them out over the sign and pressed hard. Then, satisfied with the results, he went into the dining room and washed his hands in the bubbler, went through the line, and stood by the cash register, his tray balanced against his stomach and quivering like a divining rod while he looked around the room. When he found the woman who'd told him to leave the day before, he strode over and sat beside her.

"I didn't catch your name yesterday," he said, dropping his

tray onto the table, "but I wanted to tell you you reminded me of one of my tattoos." He pulled his T-shirt up over his belly, exposing a fish that crossed his stomach. His navel formed the eye, a ball of chartreuse lint in it looking like a diseased pupil. "A pretty good likeness, don't you think?"

"*You* are disgusting," she said, and got up to leave. He watched her march away, back stiff, fists pumping.

"Mind if I eat your lunch if you're done with it?" he said to her retreating back. He pulled her tray across the table. "You should eat your vegetables. It might relieve that constipation!" The three other women at the table got up and left. He took an extra long lunch just to be sure everyone understood that he was as good as any of them. If they didn't think so they'd have to tell him to his face. He knew none of them had the guts.

Back up on the beams, he saw the nurse come out with Robinson and somebody in a suit and point him out. He could tell it was the nurse by the way she walked. He worked the rest of the shift, not even coming down for his break, figuring he could use the money. When the whistle sounded he took one last look around the countryside, lingering over the house he'd hoped to buy, trying to burn its memory into his mind: the tall windows, the copper roof, the cattails beyond it swaying in the breeze. All the way down the elevator he took in great lungfuls of the crane's diesel exhaust, enjoying its familiar tang.

Robinson was waiting for him when he got out of the elevator, his mouth set, his fists balled; his eyes didn't waver from Bolen's.

"You're a dumb shit, Bolen," he said, shaking his head. Bolen had to look down. "A good worker, but you're going to get yourself in a lot of trouble pulling stunts like that. I expected more from you." He slapped a yellow envelope into Bolen's gut and walked away.

Inside was a paycheck. Robinson had included an extra five hundred dollars and a note: "All white people are cross-grained." Bolen called out to thank him, but Robinson didn't even wave in acknowledgment.

For the next two days Bolen stalked the parking lot during shift changes until he spotted the nurse getting out of a car, a green four-door Chevy. Simple and straightforward, just like her. She probably changed her oil every three thousand miles.

That afternoon he poured a pound bag of sugar into the gas tank, then panicked when he saw her coming. He knew she'd get suspicious if he ran, so he hid under her car and grabbed her ankles and tripped her when she stopped to get her keys from her purse. She passed out from fear. He waited until she came around again, crouching above her, feeling the heat rise in waves from the pavement against his cheekbones.

"Remember me?" he asked, bending closer to her face as her eyelids blinked open. Her blue eyes grew huge and she flicked some cinders from the corner of her mouth with her tongue. "Look at me now so you don't forget my face. I'll never be far away." He patted her wrist. She kept her body rigid. "Just you keep that in mind."

Then he beat it out of town, heading east, windows open and the radio blaring, with enough money to last six or seven

months if he was careful. He hadn't really paid her back—
she'd need a new engine and fuel line if everything went according to plan, but that really wouldn't cost too much.
Besides, her insurance would pay for everything but the de-
ductible, and she seemed just the type to have a small one,
due to a good driving record. Smudging up that record was
an added benefit, though not a big one. The best part was
that he hadn't buckled under and that she'd never forget him.

He tried not to look in the rearview mirror at the familiar landscape disappearing behind him. What did it matter if
he'd liked it? His next job would be someplace to settle
down in for sure.

Back home again

For three nights Bolen slept in an abandoned farmhouse just off Route 20, eating the last of his food and staying out of the rain. Across the road a red barn leaned in a weedy field, a hand-painted sign nailed to one of its tumbledown doors: ROAD TROUBLE? CALL WORBOYS' TEXACO: 422-7070. During his days and nights in the farmhouse, listening to the wind rustle through the leaves of the surrounding oaks and the rain rattling on the tin roof, Bolen stared at the sign and began to formulate a plan. Now, with five dollars left in his pocket, driving along in the cool dusk with one elbow out the window and his last beer nearly empty on the seat beside him, he kept his eyes open for the station. The lighted Texaco sign appeared through a break in the trees, its red star shining, and he smiled; just as he'd hoped, the place looked deserted. He'd lock the attendant in the bathroom, help himself to the day's receipts and a tankful of gas, and be across the state line before anyone knew what had happened.

He turned off his engine and coasted up to the pumps. The bell rang in the station, and he saw a thirtyish, sandy-haired man crawl out from beneath a car in the first bay and head toward him, wiping his hands on his overalls. His boots crunched over the gravel. Bolen's throat tightened and sweat started on his back; he squeezed the wheel so hard his hands tingled.

"Evening," the attendant said, leaning down by his window, and Bolen read his name, F. T. Worboys, written in yellow thread above the red-and-white Texaco logo on his shirt.

"What can I do for you?" Worboys asked, studying Bolen's tattoo-covered arms.

"Seen your signs all up and down the road." Bolen reached to pop the hood release. "Saved my money till I got here. Fill her up with regular, and put a couple quarts of thirty-weight in the engine."

"You don't have to keep your foot on the brake," Worboys said, walking around to the back and tapping the taillight with the nozzle. "Car won't go anywhere while it's off." It was an old sky blue Plymouth Fury with mismatched fenders.

Bolen realized he was pressing the pedal from nervousness. He'd never done anything like this before, but now, out of money and with no job prospects, he didn't see other options. He'd made mistakes that had brought him to this point, and he knew it was unfair that others should have to pay for them, but that didn't trouble him too much. He'd been paying for other people's mistakes long enough.

He released the pedal and looked around the station. It was old—wooden, with a rusty weathervane on top of a decorative cupola, and two or three small ramshackle barns beyond it, then fields stretching to scrubby timber all around—and it was deserted. He could feel his heart thumping, and his breathing came fast and shallow. Time seemed to speed up and wind down all at once, as if he were rushing toward something in slow motion.

Worboys raised the hood and Bolen was just about to get out when a brown sheriff's car rolled slowly onto the lot. The deputy waved to Worboys, looked Bolen over, then picked up his radio and called in Bolen's license plate. Bolen released the door handle, sat back in his seat, and exhaled. They couldn't get him for anything, but Bolen knew small-town cops like this one. He'd been hassled by plenty—one just the week before. The cop had pushed him around a bit in order to feel big, then told him not to stop in his town because there was no motel, no jobs, and no rocks for him to crawl under.

The cop's radio squawked and he looked back at Bolen and held his gaze for a few seconds, then smiled and nodded and drove off more slowly than he'd come in. Robbery was out of the question. The cop had his license plate and would probably park a mile up the road, waiting for him to pass, hoping to nail him for speeding.

Bolen spit out the window. He heard crickets singing nearby and, farther off, an owl hooting in the woods. The place really was isolated. If it hadn't been for that cop he would have been golden.

In a lower corner of the station's front window a black-board hung crookedly, the words HELP WANTED scrawled in green chalk. He decided to take a chance. If it worked, his plan would be delayed, not ruined.

Worboys dropped the hood and tested it to be sure it had caught. Satisfied, he topped off the gas tank and said, "That's fifteen seventy-five."

"I can't pay," Bolen said, looking over the hood at a line of trees.

"What do you mean?"

"I mean I don't have any money." Bolen turned to Worboys.

"Then what the hell are you buying gas for?"

"I guess I'm not, unless you want to give me work." He pointed at the sign.

Worboys rubbed the back of his neck while he thought it over. He'd fired someone just the week before and was working two shifts himself plus every weekend, and he probably couldn't get anyone else since he didn't pay very well. Danny Noonan, a high school kid, worked a couple of hours each night, so he could break for dinner, and every Saturday morning, but the kid's father wouldn't let him put in more hours until his grades got better.

Bolen didn't look promising. His backseat was jammed with overflowing garbage bags of clothes, boxes of hand tools, cartons of dusty books. A drifter. Well, it wouldn't be bad to have a bit of company on the night shifts, and he wouldn't have to pay him much.

Bolen saw Worboys gauging him and knew he found him

wanting. It didn't matter. Most people did. Worboys was just another person he'd have to prove wrong. He flexed his fingers on the wheel.

"All right," Worboys said, doing some quick calculations. "Minimum wage for two months. If you stay past that I bump it a buck an hour. I pay every Friday for the week's work and I don't give advances."

The guy wouldn't last long enough to earn the raise.

"Done," Bolen said. He didn't plan on sticking around to pick up more than one or two paychecks. But one way or another, Worboys would remember him when he was gone.

He drove his Fury over to the side of the station. Worboys followed, and as Bolen got out Worboys said, "You know anything about cars?"

"I can start them." He knew more than that but it didn't suit his purposes to let on.

"Want to learn?"

"Sure."

"All right. You work the same shifts I do."

He pointed out the pumps. "If a car comes, you pump the gas. Otherwise, you can help me with whatever I'm working on." He kicked one of Bolen's tires. "We might as well start on this piece of crap until something else shows up. It's not much of an advertisement for the place. I'll take my labor out of your wages and you can buy parts at cost."

Bolen nodded. Worboys figured he wouldn't end up paying Bolen much of anything. He thumbed a dent on the hood, pushing out flakes of rust. "You sleep in this car?"

"Yes."

"Park it out back, then. When you're done, come on into

the third bay. I got a grill set up and I'll put on a couple of steaks. You look like you could use a meal."

Worboys dragged the grill across the floor to the bay entrance and started a fire, coughing as the smoke swirled around him. He brought both chairs from the office and two beers from the refrigerator and sat drinking by the open bay door, looking out over the fields. The grass was bleached yellow in the station's lights, a foot tall already and starting to choke the last of the spring's purple wildflowers. The oak trees, blackened from days of rain, were beginning to leaf, and the final pink traces of daylight showed through their upper branches.

"Where you from?" Worboys asked when Bolen came and took a seat.

"Here and there." Nervous, Bolen didn't want to say much. Robbery wasn't the career path he'd planned to follow, and he was afraid his voice might give him away. He opened his beer and inspected the bays. There was little of value—a compressor, sets of tools, a couple of radios. If he was going to get anything from this job it would have to be cash.

"Nice tattoos," Worboys said, pointing to them with the bottle. He never liked them himself but he recognized good work and Bolen's arms were covered, right down to his fingertips: bright colors, neat lines, vivid scenes. "Where'd you get them?"

"Here and there," Bolen repeated evenly, turning to meet Worboys' gaze. Behind his wire-rim glasses Bolen's eyes were gray and expressionless, and, looking at them, Worboys had the odd sensation that he was seeing the inside of a tube. It spooked him.

He picked up a stick and stirred the coals. The flames shot up briefly, and old fat coating the side of the grill sizzled and smoked, giving off an acrid smell. Bolen obviously wasn't going to be much in the way of company but Worboys decided that was all right. He could be quiet as the grave as long as he didn't steal.

Bolen leaned against the door frame, shirtless, his face tilted toward the noon sun. Danny Noonan sat in the office chair, surreptitiously studying his own reflection in the window, trying to see changes in his arms from the two hundred push-ups he did every morning. Now and then he snuck a glance at Bolen's tattoos.

"Those things hurt?" he finally asked.

"Nope," Bolen said, pulling at one of an eagle attacking a snake. "Not at all."

"I mean when you got them," Danny said, blushing.

"Nope." Bolen had seen that look of admiration before. After he'd punched his stepfather all his friends looked up to him because they wanted to pop their dads, too, but he was the only one to do it. "Ought to get yourself a couple," Bolen said, tracing the outline of a yellow tiger on his abdomen with his finger. He contracted his muscles and made the tiger ripple. "The girls like 'em."

A car cruised into the lot and ran over the hose, ringing the bell. Bolen blinked in the sun for a few seconds before he could see clearly. When he did, he pushed Danny back into the chair. "I'll get it," he said.

It was the deputy from a couple of nights before, no longer

in uniform but with an air of superiority, driving a ten-year-
old brown Ford Fairlane with a rotten muffler and nearly
bald tires. Something about the deputy's scrubbed face reminded Bolen of a nurse he'd once had a run-in with. "What
can we do for you, Deputy Dawg?"

The deputy, who'd been smiling, stepped out of the car
and asked, "What did you say?"

Danny came to the station door to listen.

Bolen, already unscrewing the gas cap, looked up and
said, "Why, I asked what kind of gas you wanted. Premium,
No Premium, or No Holds Barred?"

The deputy took off his hat and twirled it by the brim.
"What's your name, wiseguy?"

"Well now." Bolen flipped on the gas and straightened up,
one hand on his hip. "I thought you were a *dee-tective*. Can't
you figure that out on your own?"

Danny laughed and the deputy turned to him.

"What are you laughing at, Danny?"

"Nothing, sir." He dropped his head.

"What's this joker's name?" He pointed his hat at Bolen.

Danny scuffed the toe of his sneaker at a bottle cap caught
halfway under the door.

"Danny. I don't want to have to talk to your father about
this."

Danny looked up at Bolen, two pink spots blooming high
on his cheeks. Bolen smiled at him and nodded.

"*Danny*. Your father's going to be mighty angry."

"Bolen," Danny said.

"What? I can't hear you."

"*Bolen!*"

"That's better." He faced Bolen, who shut off the gas and jiggled the nozzle in the tank.

"See," Bolen said. "I knew you could do it. That'll be eight even." He screwed the gas cap on with a flourish and wiped his hands with a rag.

"What will?"

"The gas."

"How'd you know what to put in?"

"Hi-test," Bolen said, patting the car's fender. "After all, this is a high-performance baby, isn't it?"

"Listen, fuckwad," the deputy said, taking a step closer to him. "You want trouble, I'll be happy to give it to you."

He got in the car and slammed the door. "Put it on our tab."

He peeled out, kicking up dust and a spray of gravel that clicked off the station's window. Bolen, who'd stepped behind the pump, wasn't touched by it.

"We'll fix that sucker," Danny said, coughing and rubbing his eyes. Red marks freckled his cheeks where he'd been struck by gravel.

"How's that?" Bolen said, squinting after the car.

"I don't know. A nail in one of his tires next time he stops for a fill-up, maybe."

Worboys came out of a bay, wearing goggles and holding a welding torch. He'd been working on the muffler of a pickup.

"What was all that about?" he said, pointing at the cloud of dust trailing behind the deputy's car. He pulled the goggles down to his throat, leaving white circles around his eyes.

"Deputy Dawg left in an awful hurry," Bolen said. "Chasing his own tail, I guess."

Worboys looked at Danny for clarification, but he was grinning stupidly and Worboys told them both to knock it off. Bolen gave a mock salute and turned away. Danny got a broom and began sweeping the gravel off the base of the pumps.

Worboys went back into the first bay, put the torch on a long metal bench, and headed out to one of the barns. Bolen followed him a few minutes later.

Worboys stood at a worktable, polishing a wooden hand plane with a chamois cloth soaked in lemon oil. The scent made Bolen's nose itch. Worboys rubbed the plane in a circular motion, moving from one end to the other. When he finished, he flipped the plane over and started again. The care he took reminded Bolen of the way his stepfather had been with the decorative eggs displayed on their mantel at home. He whacked Bolen on the side of the head whenever he found him near them, telling him he was bound to break them. Bolen smashed every one before he left town for good.

The lemon oil kept scratching at Bolen's nose; finally, it made him sneeze.

Worboys looked up at him, startled. He seemed embarrassed to be caught taking such care with the plane, which he covered with the cloth.

"Hey, chief," Bolen said. "I think we got a problem with one of our Indians."

Worboys stood and pushed Bolen out the door, then shut and locked it behind him.

"Next time don't come in there without asking me." He

pocketed the keys and took a few steps away. "Now what's this about?"

Bolen leaned against the door. "Our boy out there." He pointed at Danny, carrying a case of oil across the gravel toward the pumps. "He wants to flatten the deputy's tire."

"What?"

"That's right. The deputy said he was going to talk to Danny's father about him, and now Danny's all hot under the collar."

Worboys watched Danny stacking the quarts of oil in the display stands on the islands, his last job before clocking out for the day. He was a good worker, always finding ways to fill up his time, but with Bolen around, he'd taken to sitting in the office and shooting the breeze.

Worboys started back toward the station with Bolen right behind him.

"And what are you telling me this for?" Worboys said, still watching Danny.

"Just protecting all our jobs."

Worboys looked at him, suddenly interested, like a cat who's detected movement in the corner of a room.

Bolen's face was blank but he knew he had Worboys' attention now. They ducked into the first bay.

"We don't want no trouble with the law," Bolen said. He dragged his fingertips through the dust on top of the pay phone, inspected them, and showed them to Worboys. "They start sniffing around in one place, they might find dirt in lots of others."

"And just what's that supposed to mean?"

"Just that there's all sorts of dirt around here." Bolen

wiped his hands on his shirt. "Jacking the pumps. Squirting oil on shocks to make it seem they're leaking. Selling empty quarts of oil, putting the nozzle in the bottom of the can the second time around."

Worboys had been careful not to let Bolen in on those tricks, and that meant either someone else had or Bolen had seen him doing it. He picked up the torch and turned a knob on its stem, which let the gas escape with a hiss, then clicked the flint twice, sparking it, and the gas jet burst into a thin blue flame. "I'll talk to him about it," Worboys said. He put his goggles on and went back to work on the rusty undercarriage of the truck. Bolen stood in the door frame, watching him with his arms crossed, and Worboys wondered how long it would be before he tried something.

Worboys sifted through the musty books in the back of Bolen's car. A shadow fell across them. Without looking up, Worboys said, "Howdy, Bolen."

"What are you doing in my car?"

Worboys ignored him. "You think you're going to be smart if you read these?" He held up one of the books. The spine read: THE HARVARD SIX FOOT SHELF OF BOOKS.

Bolen ripped it from his hands. "Don't go through my things."

"Your things?" Worboys dug a wrench out from beneath another book. "This looks like mine."

"I was using it to work on my car. Like you said I should."

"That's right. I did. But I was looking for it to work on another."

He pushed past Bolen, who made his shoulder rigid so it knocked Worboys off balance.

"Next time," Bolen said, "ask."

"Next time," Worboys said, slapping the wrench into his palm, "put my tools back. I know where every one of them belongs." He spit a stream of tobacco juice by Bolen's boot. "See, if the cops come sniffing around, it's going to be tough explaining how my tools got in your car."

Bolen smiled. Worboys had taken his bait.

A few days later Danny was moping around the garage, glaring at Bolen whenever he saw him. Worboys had yelled at him, telling him to forget any stupid ideas he might have about doing in the deputy's car, and to stick with what he'd learned. He also told him to stop puppying after Bolen.

"He'll only get you into trouble."

Worboys was cooking supper out by his shed and Bolen sat in the good office chair, feet up on the desk, watching Danny. Outside, the sun had set. A strip of orange light glowed on the horizon.

"What's with you?" Bolen asked. "You look like someone cut your balls off."

"Nothing." Danny picked up a broom and began sweeping out the office, which he'd already done half an hour before.

Bolen dropped his feet from the desk and trapped the broom against the wall.

"What? Are you pissed off about that thing with the deputy?"

He could tell he'd guessed right by Danny's silence.

"Well, don't pout. Worboys overheard you when he came out of the bay to see what was going on. I told him it was me who brought it up first and that it was just a joke, but he wouldn't go for it."

As Danny was about to jerk the broom free Bolen put his feet back up on the table. Danny pushed it sullenly at some dust balls under the cigarette machine. "He told me you blabbed."

Bolen jumped to his feet. "That son of a bitch! If he was here right now I'd call him a liar to his face."

Danny's face brightened. "Really?"

"That Worboys is a real fox." Bolen shook his head. "You got to watch him every minute." He fished around in his front pocket and pulled out his key ring, then selected a round hollow one and gave it to Danny.

"That's the key to the soda machine. Get two cream sodas from the back—they're the coldest."

"Does Worboys know you have this?"

"Hell no! Just you. I made a duplicate in town."

They drank for a while and then Bolen asked what Worboys had in the barns that was so interesting.

"Junk. Plain old junk. License plates from the thirties and forties, some old magazines and newspapers, tools—hand planes with the owners' names stamped in the wooden handles. There's three beer bottles from a hundred and fifty years ago and the sign from the original owner of this gas station. He finds things in those barns, and in the fields around here, and in the old farmhouses all along Route Twenty." He turned the broom bristle-side up, then leaned it against the wall. "Whenever he goes out cruising with the wrecker he looks into those places, sees what he can find. I don't know, the shit makes him happy.

"See that license plate over the door?" Danny pointed it out with the can. It was from Indiana, with five digits on it—13317. "That's the station's zip code, and Worboys was born in Indiana. When the guy drove in here a year ago, Worboys wanted to buy the plates from him and the guy held out for two hundred and fifty bucks. Worboys paid. Said he wouldn't eat steak for six months, but it would be worth it."

Danny took two more sodas from the machine, then tossed Bolen the keys. "There's two of those plates. He keeps the other one in the shed somewhere, in case this one's ever stolen."

"I suppose it means something to him if he's a Hoosier," Bolen said, eyeing the license plate. "But why the hell anyone would want to commemorate this place is beyond me."

"Not your kind of place?" Worboys said, coming into the office.

Startled, Danny stood up and knocked over the broom. It clattered on the floor.

"It's all right, Danny," Worboys said. "You and lover boy don't have to worry. I won't tell anyone about you."

He sat on a stack of oil cases pushed against the wall.

"I suppose an educated man like you wouldn't be happy here," he said to Bolen. He worked a stick and a pocket knife from his overalls and began whittling, stripping the bark in long peels that curled at his feet.

"That's right," Bolen said. "Look at you. Killing yourself for nothing out here, putting everything you got into a station that's bound to fail. I plan on making my money easy."

"What do you need money for? More tattoos?"

"A house," Bolen said. He regretted it instantly.

"A house." Worboys laughed. "Who'd sell you a house?" He nodded at the Fury. "You probably don't even own that car."

Bolen turned to Danny. "I got my plans. You should, too. And someplace to get them going, like Boston. That's where the money is. An old buddy of mine was working there on a roofing crew, pulling down fifty thousand a year as a fore-man. You know what foremen do, Danny?"

Danny shook his head.

"Nothing. They sit around all day in trailers reading mag-azines and eating lunch, and once every hour or two they go out and tell people what to do."

"Well you ought to be good at that," Worboys said, lean-ing forward on the stack of oil cases. "About all I've seen you do around here is find the most comfortable chair."

"Just preparing to be a foreman. All you got to do is show them you're smart and they'll make you one on the spot."

"That leaves you out right there."

Worboys checked the sharpness of the knife blade on his thumb, then went back to his whittling. "I suppose next you're going to tell me there's thousands of construction companies just waiting to hire you."

"That's right. When they see I'm a skilled worker they'll snap me up."

"Then how come you're here," he said, pointing the knife at the floor, "and not there?" He waved the knife at the win-dow. "Why hasn't this buddy of yours already hired you?"

Bolen shrugged. "He's not in construction anymore."

"What's he do now, stamp license plates for the state of Massachusetts at three cents an hour?"

"He's going through drug rehab."

"That figures."

"I'm telling you, Danny," Bolen said, ignoring Worboys, "it's crazy to think about doing anything else. Even laborers make seventeen an hour, just for moving boards." He stood by the doorway looking outside. A flock of swallows spun and dove above the treetops in the dusk, and the warm, dusty smell of the fields drifted toward him from across the road. "Think of it. That's about thirty-five grand a year. You can buy a new truck, cash. You can rent a big apartment downtown and still have enough in two years to buy yourself a house. Hell, if you want, you can work a few years and come back to this cow town and buy the biggest house around and never work again. In the meantime, there's bars in the city where a hundred new girls come in every night and restaurants you can get breakfast in twenty-four hours a day."

"You can do that here," Danny said. "Down on the Thruway, just before exit twenty-four."

Bolen wheeled on him. "You don't get it, do you? I'm not talking about driving forty-five minutes to eat greasy pancakes some ex-con burns for you. I'm talking about walking around the corner and dropping twenty bucks on a breakfast a French chef whips up on the spot. And you know something?" He leaned closer to Danny, so their faces were almost touching. "The food is so good you'd beg him to let you pay more."

Worboys snorted. "Jesus, Bolen, you got a bad case of it."

He looked at Danny, who sat with his mouth slightly open, overcome by the vision Bolen had described. "Don't tell me you *believe* him."

"Why shouldn't he? It's the truth."

"Because you're making less than he is right now," Worboys said, pointing the knife at him. "But I forgot." Worboys glanced up at Bolen from under his cap. "You've got a plan, those books of yours."

He paused and Bolen shifted in the doorway, trying to figure out what he was driving at.

"I looked through them the other day. Says it's supposed to be a six-foot stack. But you're missing more than half." Worboys sent a strip of bark flying with the knife. "I guess that makes you about two-foot-six."

Danny laughed.

"You're pretty funny, aren't you, Poorboys?" Bolen said.

"That's right." Worboys dropped his hands to his lap. "I am."

"Give me one good reason why Danny should listen to you," Bolen said.

"Why should he listen to a thirty-year-old burnout?"

"Thirty-one, to be exact," Bolen said.

"At least I own this place," Worboys said. "And I don't have stupid ideas about buying any houses."

"You own this place. Great. Like that's a character reference." Bolen kicked a wall. "I could go out and buy an acre of dog turds that would be worth as much."

He turned to Danny. "I been waiting a long time for my time to come, and when it finally does, it'll be some kind of sweet."

Worboys stood and dusted off his thighs. "Forget about him, Danny. He's a fool." He watched a car's headlights approaching in the distance. "And the name's Worboys," he said, to Bolen.

"Poorboys, Worboys, what's the difference?"

"Keeping your job, that's the difference."

He thought about making Bolen say his name and that he understood, but decided it wasn't worth it. Bolen had that hollow look to his eyes and Worboys didn't want to push him too far. Not yet, anyway. If he got another week from Bolen he'd be happy, and then he'd tell him to shove off. Danny's friends would be out of school and one of them was bound to want some work.

The car rolled to a stop by the pumps. The brake lights flickered and went off. A pretty woman with long blond hair and bright red lipstick was driving, and Worboys had never seen her before.

Danny hopped up.

"Leave it be, Danny. I'll service her. Looks like she could use a man."

"Then why are you going?" Bolen said.

Worboys smiled down at him. "I'll let you have that one."

He folded up his knife and walked toward the car.

Bolen opened the soda machine and took out two more sodas. He pocketed a fistful of quarters.

"I'll tell you what," he said, pacing from wall to wall in the office. He watched Worboys talking to the woman under the station lights. "Let's play a little trick on old Poorboys there. What time's your shift start tomorrow?"

"Six o'clock. I go from six to nine."

"Make it a little later." He shook the soda and swallowed the foam in one gulp, then tossed the can on the oil cases stacked in the corner.

"At about seven-thirty call up and tell him you lost track of the time. Your car won't start and you've been working on it for a while. Ask him to come and give you a ride."

"I don't know," Danny said, picking up Bolen's can and throwing it in a trash barrel. It rattled against the metal sides. "He's liable to get awful pissed."

"What?" Bolen said, turning away from the window to stare at him. "Are you afraid? You think you're going to lose this job?"

"Well, it's just that he's got big plans for the garage, which means big plans for me." Danny couldn't resist a smile. "He's going to make me assistant manager pretty soon."

"When'd he tell you this?"

"Just the other day."

"That figures. Don't you see? He can tell you're starting to realize this place isn't so great."

"What do you mean?"

"I mean don't waste your time waiting." Bolen pointed at the Indiana plate over the door. "Who gives a fuck about Indiana and this zip code? Nobody. And if it doesn't mean anything to anybody else it's never going to make him money. That's your boy's problem in a nutshell. And if you stick with him, it's going to be yours."

Danny studied his shoes, unconvinced.

"Or how about that woman?"

"What about her?"

"She's the first one to stop by in half an hour. This isn't exactly a prime location. In two years this place won't even be here."

"Then why'd he hire you?"

"He has to sleep sometimes. It's the same with you. You come and he knocks off for dinner, you leave and he sits up another five hours, watching the road and hoping somebody will show up. You may not know this place is folding but you can bet your bottom dollar he does."

"You think so?"

Danny watched him pace, waiting for his response, and Bolen could tell that the possibility had never occurred to him. He looked like a kid who'd just discovered that the world wasn't perfect and now had to decide whether or not to accept the truth.

Bolen moved to the door and stood staring out at the road that led to town, its pavement turning purple in the fading evening light. "You want to spend the rest of your life like this? Nothing to do on a Saturday but listen to the crickets and get drunk in a bar and fight the same guys you fought the week before?"

Danny went to the window and silently raised and lowered the window shade. He looked at Bolen's reflection, his tattooed arms.

"I don't know. Canajoharie's a pretty good town."

"Canajoharie? You call that a town?"

"It sure is. It used to be a great one," Danny said, shifting his feet with eagerness. "It used to be a mill town, and it used to have an opera house, lots of things."

"Listen to you. 'Used to be this, used to be that.' That's

exactly what that place is, a used-to-be town." He snorted his disgust. "Now tell me again, is this how you want to spend your life?"

Danny didn't answer.

"I didn't think so." Bolen headed for the bay door. "Listen, it's just going to be a little joke. That's the way we get along. He jokes about me, I joke with him. Worboys can take it. Besides, it's not going to be anything serious. Maybe I'll short-sheet his bed or put toothpaste in his socks. If he blows up, you can come with me when I leave."

"You mean it?"

"Sure. Count on it." He rapped his knuckles on the door frame. "We'll make big bucks together."

Worboys leaned his chair back against the brick wall of the station, listening to the baseball game on the radio and sipping a Coke for the caffeine. The Red Sox were playing the Yankees up in Boston, where it was threatening rain. Here the evening star glowed in a clear blue-green sky, just above the trees on the horizon, and a few last birds called to each other through the gathering dark.

Worboys watched the road for Danny's truck and counted passing cars. Every now and then customers pulled in, mostly teenagers, wired up on dates and wearing too much cologne, and two couples an hour apart he was sure were married to other people. He could tell by the way their hands suddenly left their laps at the sound of his approaching steps and the way they sat, too close together for middle-aged people with wedding rings.

Worboys had a lot of time to speculate on these things and

that bothered him. It meant he didn't have enough customers. And now he had to worry about Bolen and Danny.
The kid was beginning to believe some of the stupid things
Bolen told him, which galled Worboys, and tonight he was
an hour late for his shift. Worboys' stomach growled from
the wait for dinner. And when Worboys had asked Bolen to
sit outside with him he'd refused. That was strange.

Worboys looked up at the fish-eye mirror outside the
first bay. He'd put it there ostensibly to make sure no one
got run over or cracked into a car when backing out, but
from where he sat it also allowed him to keep an eye on the
office. Bolen walked to the door and stood with his head
tilted to one side, listening, then reached behind the register—an old-fashioned, hand-operated one—pinched the
bell between his fingers, and punched the NO SALE key, opening the drawer. He didn't take much, five, maybe ten dollars, Worboys couldn't see the denomination, but that
wasn't the point. If he'd been doing this for a while he probably had quite a stash for himself, and no doubt planned on
taking off. And if he was willing to chance it he'd probably
clean out the register the night he left, too.

After fifteen minutes Bolen came out to join him,
whistling and dragging the good chair through the gravel.
Pebbles stuck in the coasters. That was another sign Bolen
planned to make some kind of break. Worboys had told him
before not to bring that chair out, and now Bolen no longer
even pretended to care what Worboys thought.

"I guess I'll take you up on that offer," Bolen said. "It's too
hot in the office to even think about watching TV." He sat
down and popped the top on his beer. "Who's winning?"

"Sox. Top of the sixth, three to one. Clemens is throw-ing heat tonight. Twelve strikeouts already."

They listened to the game—the roar of the crowd and the quiet tock of the bat hitting the ball—and to the crickets chirping around them, and watched the crescent moon come up through the trees, climbing like a bright bird from branch to branch. Bolen's chair creaked whenever he sat forward.

The phone rang and Worboys went into the office to an-swer it. It was Danny, asking for a ride. He'd left the lights on in his car overnight and couldn't get a jump.

Worboys took the money from the register, folded it in half, and stuffed it in his front pocket. He checked the read-ings on all the pumps, then went into the bay and backed out the truck. Hopping down, he told Bolen he had to go into town. Bolen leaned his chair back against the bricks.

Worboys suddenly turned and flipped the chair from be-neath Bolen with his foot and before Bolen could stand punched him behind the ear. Then he kneeled on Bolen's back and pushed his face in the gravel. Holding his head down, he could feel a trickle of warm blood through Bolen's stringy hair.

"You think I'm too stupid to see what you did inside?" He didn't wait for Bolen to answer. "Now, I know how much those pumps read and I know how much money there is in that drawer, and when I come back there better be ten dol-lars more in it than the amount of gas you've sold while I'm gone. And then we're going to go through your car to make sure you don't have anything that doesn't belong to you and when we're done you'll get in it and clear out of town. Oth-erwise I'm going to the sheriff and report that you've been stealing money all along. I don't know whether you have, but it doesn't matter. I'll make the charges stick. You got that?"

Bolen heaved his back, trying to get up, and Worboys kneed him in the side. He ground Bolen's face in the gravel again, causing him to grunt.

"You got it?"

"You go to the sheriff with that and I'll tell him what I know," Bolen said.

"Go right ahead. You won't have anybody to back you up. If you think Danny will, you're crazy." He pushed Bolen's face a little further into the gravel. "Now, one last time. You got it?"

"Yes."

"All right then." Worboys stood and when Bolen got to his hands and knees kicked him in the stomach and then the hip, so he couldn't get up fast and come after him. Bolen curled on his side on the ground.

"You just stay there for a minute while I finish my business."

Worboys took a pipe wrench from his pocket. He opened the hood of Bolen's car and cracked the distributor cap, then checked through the parts boxes in the back of the second bay until he found the two distributor caps he had for Plymouths. He came back and put his boot on the knuckles of one of Bolen's outstretched hands and shifted his weight onto it until Bolen grunted in pain.

"See these?" He held out the distributor caps.

Bolen nodded and tried to pull his hand free. Worboys pressed harder. He tossed the pipe wrench into the bay; it clattered on the pavement. "They fit your car. I'll give you one when I get back." He lifted his boot. "Free of charge."

Bolen rinsed his face in the double sink. The rusty taste of blood filled his mouth. He thought about sticking around and seeing who could convince the sheriff, but Worboys was probably right. Danny was too much of a sheep to count on. It didn't matter. Bolen had been lifting parts for his car all along, hiding them in the tall grass behind Worboys' shed. He had no problem fixing his car. He'd stashed a distributor cap just the day before and it took him only fifteen minutes to install.

He grabbed all the tools he needed, and some he didn't, and most anything else he could fit in his car including the compressor, but he wanted to do something else, too, something that would really hurt Worboys. He wanted Worboys to remember how badly he'd underestimated him whenever he thought of it. Bolen stood outside the station a long time before he figured out what to do.

He picked up the pipe wrench Worboys had dropped and smashed all the panes in the bay window. The sound of the shattering glass made him happy, like he was a kid opening a bunch of brightly colored Christmas presents all at once. Then he filled a jerrican with gasoline and poured it on the grass around the barn where Worboys kept everything he'd collected, lighted it, and left the station, heading east for Boston.

He hadn't gotten what he wanted out of the deal, but Worboys hadn't gotten much from him, either. There was some satisfaction in that. Plus he could use the tools to find other work, and the compressor would bring a couple of hundred, fast. He watched the fire burning in his rearview mirror until he rounded a corner and it turned into a yellow glow above the black trees. He'd be across the state line before Worboys even called it in.

The barn was still burning fiercely, gushering up into the night sky in the distance like a giant torch when Worboys came back from town with Danny.

"You're fired," he said, without looking at Danny.

Worboys cut through a field, bumping over the old railroad ties he'd placed around the gravel to keep it from spreading, and shut off the engine and hopped down from the cab while the truck was still rolling. The flames sucked up oxygen with a great whooshing sound and even from fifty feet Worboys felt the heat through his clothes, as if they were being pressed by an iron. His eyebrows prickled with the beginnings of a singeing.

He told Danny to call in the fire and grabbed an extinguisher from the rear of the truck and ran toward the flames before realizing the extinguisher would be worthless. He flung it at the fire and ran back and got a hose, and for the next twenty minutes he soaked the grass around the burning building. Just before the firemen arrived the building collapsed in on itself, sending out a groundswell of sparks and glowing coals that hissed and sputtered as they swept over the dampened grass. A cloud of steam billowed around Worboys, momentarily blinding him, and when he could see again the grass behind him was burning. He thought the whole place would blow.

He was stamping on the flames when a fireman pushed him aside; it was Tim Hardaway, the deputy, but Worboys didn't recognize him. He slumped on the bumper of the wrecker, head bowed, waiting for an explosion that never came, and tried not to think of everything he'd lost in the fire. It had taken him two years to gather that collection, tools and bottles and signs, and he doubted he could find many of those things again. He also had a stack of money buried in the dirt beneath the floor, but that would probably be all right. He hoped so, and hoped that Bolen hadn't found it. He picked up handfuls of gravel and let them sift through his fingers while he went through the collection piece by piece in his head.

After a long time the deputy put his hand on Worboys' shoulder to tell him the fire was out and Worboys flinched—his skin had burned right through his clothes. Not badly, but as if he'd been out in the sun for hours after not seeing it all winter, and the hair on his arms was gone.

"What happened?" Hardaway asked.

"One of my workers . . ." Worboys' words trailed off as he gestured at the smoking embers.

"That tattooed freak?"

Worboys nodded.

"Don't worry. We'll find him. I called in his plate number last week. Nancy probably still has it on tape."

He patted Worboys on the shoulder again and went to talk to some of the other firemen, who were peeling off their boots and coats. Worboys waved to thank them, too tired to talk, then trudged to his shed to sleep, his face still smudged with soot. He wondered why Bolen hadn't tried to really destroy the place. He lay down on his bed and stared up at the rust spots around the rivets on the tin roof, sure he'd missed something. Bolen wasn't the type to let it go at a simple fire.

Bolen had just raised a Boston station on his radio when he passed a cop by the side of the road. He was going sixty-two but he didn't even tap his brakes. In the dark they couldn't tell what kind of car he had, or its color; they'd be looking at his plates. And his were new, five-digit ones, their stickers all in order.

INDIANA, they read. BACK HOME AGAIN.

Worboys' Transaction

—·—·—·—·—·—·—·—·—·—

F. T. Worboys, parked twenty yards from the highway on a dusty access road, sat in the cab of his wrecker, listening for the hum of approaching cars and watching the reflected glow of his cigarette brighten and fade on the windshield as he breathed. It was two o'clock in the morning. Crickets chirped in the underbrush around him and he heard the wind pushing through the leaves of the overhanging maples and oaks like rain. He was waiting for someone to come down the road and hit the small bits of sharpened metal he'd spread over one lane of the highway. He'd placed them carefully, about fifty yards after a turn, so that whoever hit them wouldn't be going too fast when they did. From a distance, with the moonlight glinting off them, they looked like a small puddle on the macadam.

He figured he'd get at least two tires out of the deal and

maybe three; with the towing charge thrown in the bill wouldn't come to less than two hundred and fifty dollars. Business had been slow for a while. F.T. was twenty-nine and single. He knew that if he was going to make something of himself he'd have to do it soon; a man was only given so much time to work with. The metal bits were part of his continuing plan, which had begun two years before when he'd bought the Texaco station. It was on Route 20, once the main road across northern New York but nearly forgotten since the opening of the Thruway twenty miles to the north. F.T. had come across the station after working in a series of others. It was failing, and selling cheap, and he'd bought it with money he'd put aside for just that purpose. The first thing he'd done was to order new denim workshirts so that everyone who worked for him advertised the place. Written in yellow thread above the red-and-white Texaco logo, the letters raised like a fresh scar, were the words F. T. WORBOYS' TEXACO. Below the logo were the words TRUST THE MAN WITH THE STAR.

He hadn't had many workers. A couple he'd fired; a few had been drifters. He knew when he hired someone just what type he'd be. The drifters usually stood with their hands in their back pockets and their eyes focused beyond his shoulder when he talked to them, as if they were already thinking about their next job. He didn't mind; he paid them less. Some lasted longer than others. One, a tattooed nut named Bolen, had stayed only a couple of weeks. When he left, though, he'd burned down two of the old outbuildings on the place, torching tools and signs that Worboys had scavenged from the area, and had nearly cleaned out the garage, taking among other things two sets of socket wrenches, a compressor, three drills, a set of metric wrenches for foreign cars, and boxes of spare engine parts. As far as F.T. was concerned that was about as low as you could get. Stealing was one thing, taking the means of a man's livelihood another.

After that Worboys never hired another drifter and he always stood the night shift himself. He moved into a shed behind the station and set up a cot and a dresser, with a big standing fan he had bought from a junk dealer for five dollars and fixed up himself. It stirred up the hot air a little on summer nights when otherwise it wouldn't move. He'd lie awake on his bed, waiting for cars to come, crunching over the gravel toward the pumps. He had a telephone on his dresser so that if anyone called for a tow—he'd posted signs all up and down Route 20—he wouldn't have to run to the station to answer it. Almost no one ever did. One night when he was lying on his cot, listening to the mosquitoes buzz around below the tin ceiling, he'd gotten the idea for the metal.

So now he sat, one big-knuckled hand on the wheel, the other nervously tapping time on the stem of the side-view mirror. He heard a car coming, not too fast, and guessed by the pitch of its engine that it was a big American model, something with a V-8 that could unwind pretty good but that hadn't been aired out in a while. It passed the road where he waited and Worboys saw in the moonlight that it was a '72 Buick Electra, light-colored and in good shape. Ten seconds later he heard the concussive pop of its tires blowing out, followed by the squeal of its brakes, then gravel kicking up against the car's sides.

"Must have left the road," he said, throwing his cigarette out the window. The sound of his voice echoing in the cab startled him. He hadn't talked to anyone in a while. He wondered who was in the car and hoped it might be a pretty girl. He got out of the truck and walked a few steps into the woods, unzipping his pants as he went. He didn't want to appear too soon after the accident and raise any suspicions. As soon as he started pissing the crickets stopped their singing. He thought again of who was in the car. A girl, sure, and lonely and scared, out in the middle of nowhere with two flat tires. It'd be natural for her to take a liking to him. He laughed at himself, but in his hurry to get back to the truck he caught himself in his zipper.

He turned the truck around and headed off the access road to a smaller one. This one led back to the highway further up, so he could come up to the car from the other direction and not have to drive over the metal himself, or avoid it and then have to explain how he knew it was there. He drove with his shoulders bunched up and a cold sweat beginning on his back. He'd hit thirty-five by the time he reached the car. When he saw the old man bent over one of its wheels he felt like driving on by, but the man turned and saw him and Worboys pulled off the side of the road. When the dust had settled he stuck his head out the window.

"What seems to be the problem?"

Worboys guessed the man was near eighty. He was still strong, with a big round head as bald as a pumpkin. He stood next to his car, looking at Worboys, his hands in his back pockets, his jaw thrust forward. Two teeth, all he had left, stuck up into space, as if to challenge Worboys. He reminded Worboys of a cracked anvil—it couldn't take too many shots, but you wouldn't want it to drop on you.

"What are you asking me for?" the man said, and his teeth bobbed up and down a few times. "You know damn well what the problem is."

"I know?" Worboys said, looking down for a moment in spite of himself. "How the hell should I know what the problem is?"

He reminded himself to wait longer the next time.

"All my tires are blown."

"*All* of them?" Worboys was genuinely surprised.

"That's right," the man said, less belligerently. He seemed somewhat mollified by the tone of Worboys' voice. "All of them."

"Christ. It's lucky you weren't hurt."

"And I suppose it's luck that brought you here."

"Not really. I cruise this highway two or three times a night, seeing if anyone's disabled. This was my last run before getting some shut-eye."

He walked around the car once, keeping an eye on the old man, who looked like he wanted to fight, then squatted down and began rubbing his hands lightly around one of the tires. When he found pieces of the metal embedded in the rubber he pulled a few free by working them from side to side. The old man stood silently behind him, watching. He had on blue Bermuda shorts, a pressed button-down shirt, and sneakers. He looked like he'd planned on going to the beach. But a bar of dirt stretched across the shirt's front and one of its buttons was missing, and one of his shins was scraped and bloody.

"See these?" Worboys said, standing and showing him the metal. "They're in all your tires." He looked out onto the road. "Someone must have spread them on the highway."

"Must have been your twin brother," the man said, his teeth sticking up even higher.

"I don't have a brother," Worboys said, dropping the metal and dusting his hands on his overalls.

"Then it must have been you."

Worboys lowered his head and shook it sadly. He made a neat pile of the metal with the side of his boot, tensed his jaw, then looked up.

"Mister, I don't know where you're from, but around here we just don't do that kind of thing."

"Somebody did. Who was it, Peter Pan?"

"Probably kids." He squinted toward the woods. "Did you see anything after it happened?"

"I heard your truck."

"Once you get a notion you just won't let it go, will you?"

"I've got a notion to punch you right in the nose."

"Why's that?"

"Because this didn't happen five minutes ago and you're already here, ready to tow me. You might as well have parked where you are and saved the gas." He snorted. "I'll bet you've got a warehouse full of these tires just waiting for me."

"These?" Worboys said, kicking one. "Sure. I got plenty. They're standard size."

"And you expect me to believe you didn't plan this?"

"If I'd'a planned this, you'd be sixty years younger and female."

He took out a cigarette and lighted it, cupping the match from the wind. If the guy was going to swing, he figured, he'd have done it by now.

"I expect you'll believe whatever you want to. Now, how far back did you hit?"

"'Bout a hundred feet, near that puddle," he said, nodding up the road.

"Puddle?" Worboys said, starting for it. "We haven't had rain in a week."

He gathered the metal, some of which had been scattered into the other lane, and piled it beneath a roadside bush. When he came back he said, "That way no one else'll hit it, and it's there if you want to make a police report."

"Police?" the old man said, his teeth dropping back into his mouth for the first time all night. "What do I want with them?"

"A report might get you back the money from your insurance agent."

"What money?"

"The money you're going to spend on the four tires from my warehouse, plus the tow to get you there." He smiled at the old man. "Unless you carry four spares."

"No," he said, looking around, as if hoping to see someone else to bargain with. He stuck his chin out again, hesitating, and for a moment Worboys thought he was going to tell him to go to hell. Finally he sighed, the air whistling as it pushed between his teeth, his chin receded, and his hands dropped to his sides.

"All right. How much will it be?"

Worboys rolled his head upward. His lips moved as if he were counting to himself, but he already knew the total.

"Four hundred dollars. Fifty for the tow and three-fifty for the four tires."

"I only need three. I got a spare."

"Three-fifty then. They're a buck apiece, but seeing as how you're in trouble, I was going to give you a deal." He wondered how far he could push it. "You might want to take it. Getting caught out here without a spare isn't exactly a good idea."

"Some deal." He shook his head, but Worboys knew he'd take it. Getting him to agree to the tow had been the difficult part.

"Okay. Four hundred. You take Triple A?"

"Nope. They're too hard to collect from."

"How about American Express?"

"Cash or personal check."

"Who the hell's got that kind of cash?" the old man said, flaring. "And what would you do if I didn't have a check? Leave me here?"

Abruptly, he raised his trembling hands in front of his chest, then dropped them.

"Ah, the hell with you," he said, and turned away. "I don't have a check, and I don't have the money." He began inspecting one of the tires.

Worboys bounced lightly against the car, arms folded across his chest. The old guy was turning out to be tougher than he'd expected.

"All right," he said, bluffing. He climbed back up to his cab.

"I'll call the cops, tell 'em you're out here." His was the only station open for miles around. They'd just call him back and ask him to come for the tow.

"No," the old guy said, his head snapping up so fast the moonlight glinted off his glasses like a spark. "Don't call the cops. I'll be all right out here on my own."

That was the second time he'd gotten nervous about the cops: Worboys wondered what he was afraid of. He figured the barked shin had something to do with it. The car's tags were out of state, and he knew nobody went too far from home without money. Besides, he found himself liking the old man's feistiness.

"All right," he said reluctantly, swinging the door back and forth as he leaned on it. It squeaked beneath his weight.

"Just get in the truck."

"I told you I can't pay."

Jesus! Worboys thought. This guy really wants to come out on top. "Look, just get in the damn truck."

He did as he was told. Worboys reached inside the car and the smell of wine nearly knocked him over. Three full bottles clinked together on the floor. A fourth, on the seat, had dripped a purple stain. That explained some of the nervousness. Worboys whistled silently, impressed. If the guy had been drinking, he showed no signs of it. The ignition key was by itself, no trunk key, no key ring. He put the car in gear so it wouldn't roll on him when he scrambled underneath it, jockeyed the truck into position, and attached the sling. Getting into the truck, he slammed the door behind him.

"Name's F. T. Worboys," he said, starting the truck and

shoving it into gear. It bucked once as the slack went out of
the cable, rattling the tools in the toolbox, then pulled
smoothly onto the highway.

"Fred, Fred Mostone," the old man said, smiling into the
darkness.

Soon they saw the station. Its lights were ablaze, and the
sound of people talking floated toward them over the fields
and empty gravel lot surrounding it.

"Say," Fred said. "Who's that talking?"

"The radio. Keeps thieves away." He looked over at Fred,
then back at the white line along the edge of the road.

"Makes the place seem less dead when I come back to it,"
he almost added, but kept it to himself.

Fred leaned forward to look it over.

"Not too many cars you're working on."

F.T., who hadn't liked giving in to Fred back on the road,
liked this even less.

"Nope," he said, popping the emergency brake and kicking open his door. "But I got yours, and right now that's all
I need."

Worboys turned the dial to get a late-night baseball talk show,
cranked the volume to full blast, then ignited the compressor
and plugged in the pneumatic wrench's air hose. The compressor roared to life, belching a cloud of diesel smoke, and
echoing loudly in the nearly empty garage. He dragged the
wrench over to the back of the car and pried off the hubcaps
with a pinch bar. He took off all the nuts, moving counter-
clockwise from the top one, each time letting the nut come
off in the socket, then flicking it loose into the hubcap, where

it rattled around until coming to rest with the others. The wrench made a noise like a muffled jackhammer but Worboys, used to it, didn't notice. Fred snapped off the radio.

"Hey!" Worboys said. "What are you doing?"

"I can't talk with that thing on."

"Then talk."

Worboys went back to his work.

"There's easier ways of doing that."

"Like what?"

"Put it chest high and hold the wheel steady with one hand, then you won't have to bend so much."

"You a mechanic?"

"No."

"Used to be?"

"No."

"I'll do it my way then." He took off another nut. "I'd rather listen to the radio than to that kind of advice."

Fred walked around the garage, poking into open drawers and looking at the white spaces on the walls where tools and parts had hung.

"Kind of low on tools, aren't you?"

"Somebody stole 'em."

"Your radio didn't do you much good."

F.T. ignored him. Fred peered into the darkness outside the garage, then came and stood next to Worboys.

"I stole something once."

"Yeah? What was that, bubble gum?"

"This car."

"Sure. And this ain't my station. I'm only using it while the owner's out of town."

"Don't believe me?"

"Nope."

Worboys eyed him, then moved to the next wheel. He squatted, pulling the hubcap close to him; it rasped across the cement. He worked a bag of chewing tobacco from a side pocket, took a plug, and offered the bag to Fred.

"No thanks, I can't chew on account of my gums." He drew back his lips, showing F.T. his pitted gums. "Besides, I never liked that brand. I used to grow my own."

"Grew it? Where?"

"On a farm, not thirty miles down the road."

"You're shitting me," F.T. said, lowering the wrench. "You can grow tobacco in New York?"

"And just about anything else. Anyway, I could once. I don't know about now. I haven't seen the farm in a while."

Worboys, getting interested, didn't want to speak too soon. He raised the car shoulder high and removed the wheels, then rolled them against the far wall, where he pulled off the rubber with a pinch bar. He stacked it neatly; later he would sell it to the junk dealer. He pulled four new tires from an overhead rack and let them bounce on the floor. They sounded like underinflated basketballs.

While working them onto the rims and inflating them he said, "My father always wanted to be a farmer."

"What was he?"

"Old."

"How old?"

"Your age, I guess. Maybe older. He fought in World War One."

"Jesus. That is old."

"Eighty-two when he had me."

"You remember him?"

"Not really."

Worboys' friends had called him Father Time and he'd always seemed feeble to Worboys, old before Worboys was born, dead before he made much of an impression.

Worboys hoisted one of the wheels and aligned the holes with the bolts. "So why'd you steal the car?"

"Change your mind?"

"Nope. I'll listen to your story, then decide."

"It's my birthday."

Worboys laughed. "You always steal a car on your birthday?"

"No. Just this one."

Worboys started putting on the wheels.

"I done everything in my life—everything," Fred said, and when he spoke he thrust his jaw forward, as if he were ready to fight anyone who contradicted him. "Carpenter, painter, electrician. You name it. But I'm getting old." That fact seemed to have come to him as a great and sudden surprise. He lifted his hands and looked at them. "My goddamn hands shake so much that I can't even hold a screwdriver steady, and without my glasses I'm blind." He dropped his hands back onto his thighs. "But hell, I'm not helpless."

He worked his jaw for a minute. Worboys went on to the next tire.

"All my relatives came over this afternoon. Kids, grandchildren, nieces, nephews." His voice was sing-songy. "They talked about me like I was already dead. 'Give Gramps some pasta.' 'Don't let Gramps get tired.' 'Make sure Gramps doesn't drink too much wine.' Hell, I gave up drinking wine before most of them were born."

Worboys' mother had called his father "Old man," even to his face, though she wasn't young herself. He wondered now how that must have felt.

Fred kicked at a piece of scrap metal.

"Listening to them gave me a headache, so I told them I was going to lay down for a minute. I could see the car from my bed. It used to be mine, a long time ago, but I gave it to my nephew, Tommy. He's a good kid, kind of strange. Drinks by himself, won't drive the car except on nice days in the summer. Puts old newspapers in the trunk. He says he's saving it."

Fred patted the car.

"For what? I remembered I had an extra key, so I climbed out and took it."

"Just like that? No problems getting out the window?"

"Nah," Fred said, dismissing the suggestion with a wave of his hand. "Popped a button on my shirt, scraped a shin, but that's about it." He smiled. "They probably think I'm still sleeping. Didn't want to disturb me about Tommy's car."

"Freddie," Worboys said, laughing again. "You're all right. It'll be a while before you see the boneyard."

He finished putting on the last wheel, then lowered the car.

"How come you ended up here?"

"Didn't have anything in mind when I took it, but Tommy had four bottles of homemade wine on the seat, and I remembered we used to make wine up here on the farm. My wife's buried there and I wanted to see it again."

"Where exactly is this place?"

"Between here and Canajoharie."

"Another twenty miles and you'd have made it."

"I'd have made it if it hadn't been for you," Fred said, straightening.

"If it hadn't been for me, you'd have been out there all night."

Worboys coiled the hose beside the compressor and cut the switch. He started the car and slowly depressed the accelerator to the floor; finally he let the motor idle and came around and opened the hood.

"What are you up to now?" Fred asked.

"Trying to get you to your farm all right. I don't want to go to bed and then have to get up and tow you again. This thing's idling way too slow."

He took a long screwdriver and turned a screw just beneath the carburetor, first almost bringing the engine to a stop, then raising its idle until he was satisfied with the pitch. He bent over the engine and opened the carburetor. He clucked and shook his head.

"It's all gummed up. Engines like this weren't made to turn over this slowly."

"That's all right. I'll live with it. It got me this far."

Worboys got back in the car as if he hadn't heard him and held the accelerator to the floor a full two minutes. A cloud of blue smoke filled the garage and the engine's vibration bounced the screwdriver across the workbench and onto the floor. When he let up, the engine ran more smoothly.

"So how long are you going to be on this farm?"

"About a week, I guess. I'll let them worry some about

me first, and I might fix up the house before heading back to Boston."

"You going back this way?"

"I been by here once."

"Well, a week'll be plenty of time to get this running clean. Take it out every day on the highway, just for an hour or so. That'll unclog the lines and keep it out of the shop."

He picked the carburetor cap and bent to replace it, then hesitated, holding it over the engine in his upturned palm as if weighing it, and said, "I'll tell you what. You've run up a pretty big bill here. I'll throw in an oil change for free. Go on into the office there and get me a case of thirty-weight."

After Fred left, Worboys reached into the back of his toolbox for a plastic film container. Inside, rattling as he picked it up, were twenty or so BBs. He poured a couple onto his palm and picked the shiniest of the bunch; the rest he put back in the case. He held the BB above the open carburetor and as he did an image of Freddie clambering out his window rose to his mind: the old man grunting as he turtled his fat stomach over the sill, his feet searching for the ground, finally popping a button and dropping onto his unsteady legs. He was lucky he hadn't killed himself. Worboys smiled, glad he'd get the chance to see Fred again, then dropped the BB. He was just closing the hood as Fred came back into the garage with the case of oil.

When he had finished, Worboys backed the car out and pocketed the key. He was going to be gone a minute or two and didn't want Fred to clear out without paying.

"All set?" Fred asked.

"Just a minute." He went back into his shed and rummaged around. When he came back he had an extra shirt and jacket.

"Here," he said, giving them to Fred, who put the shirt on over his own. "You'll need a change of clothes there. These are all I've got."

The shirt had the Texaco logo, and F.T.'s name.

"Thanks," Fred said, looking at it. "You won't see these again."

"That's all right. You can advertise me down in Boston. And who knows? It's an old car. If you run into problems, my card is in the pocket."

"What, did you give me leaky tires?"

Worboys clapped him on the shoulder as they walked outside. The air was sharply clean after the exhaust fumes in the garage. A faint pink glow was spreading across the eastern sky and all but a few crickets had stopped their singing.

"You like fishing?" Worboys asked.

"Sure. It's been a while, but sure."

"My dad used to take me. Deep sea fishing. I loved the sound of the exhaust pipes burbling in the water, the salt-water and fish smell of the docks. The boards were slippery by the water, and I always thought I was going to fall in. We used to go this time of the morning." It was the light that had made him remember the trips, for the first time in years, and listening to Freddie's stories. But now that he'd spoken Worboys was embarrassed to have brought it up. He cleared his throat and shrugged.

Fred didn't seem to know what to make of it, either.

"I'll come right back here if those tires are bad," he said.

"I'm sure you will."

"What do I owe you?"

"Four even. No tax if I keep it off the books."

"Fine." Fred took out a checkbook.

"I thought you didn't have any checks."

"I remembered them when you threw in that oil change."

"You sure it's good?"

"Yeah, but I can always cancel it."

"That's all right," F.T. said, looking at the address. "I'll know where to come looking for you, too."

Worboys' eyes felt dry and heavy from the long night's work. He wondered if Freddie wasn't tired, too.

"You all right to drive?" he asked. "I'll make us some coffee, or you can crash here for a couple of hours." He nodded at his shed.

"Nah." He shook his head. "I want to get there soon."

"Fair enough." They shook hands and said their good-byes; Worboys gave him the key and Fred backed out of the lot.

Worboys waved, and the last thing he saw clearly, before the Buick pulled out of the station's circle of light, was his own logo shining at him from Freddie's chest.

He tried to figure out how long the BB would take to work its way through the carburetor to the manifold—a day, two at most. From there it would roll into the cylinders. At 1500 rpm's that would blow a cylinder head. There'd be plenty of money in that. Worboys went inside to check his engine parts. As he'd thought, Bolen had stolen the ones he needed. He called a twenty-four-hour auto-parts-supply place, ordered, and then, yawning and swatting at a few early morning flies, went off to bed.

IF THERE HADN'T BEEN A MONKEY IN THE CAR SHE WOULD HAVE SUNG

———·—·—·—·—·—·—·—·—·—

Lee drove five miles an hour under the speed limit, one hand on top of the monkey's cage. Her fingers were still damp from a roadside stop to cover the license plate with mud and rinse her hands in a puddle. Outside the car, the heat had been immediate and oppressive. The roadside trees looked withered in the noon sun and heat waves shimmered on the tar. The covered license plate was Lee's one concession to the fact that what she was about to do—set a wild monkey loose in her sister's ex-boyfriend's store—might be somewhat illegal. That, and that she was driving a rental car so no one could trace her, if you were counting concessions, which Lee wasn't. She was going to teach Lewis a lesson.

The monkey chattered at her the entire way from Charlotte. Every few minutes it reached through the bars of its cage and rattled the lock, and now and then it tried to grab her arm. An orange sticker pasted to the top of the cage had the words HOW TO CARE FOR ME written across it in bold black letters, with detailed instructions in smaller print underneath. Lee kept her hand on the cage because the monkey had already flipped it onto the floor once, causing her to panic and veer onto the dusty shoulder, afraid it would get loose and do its damage to the car. She wasn't surprised. At the store, it had seemed particularly feisty, tearing the newspapers lining the bottom of the cage into even strips and stuffing them through the bars while of its two companions one slept and the other sat miserably in the corner, its pink bottom stuck in a pail of water.

The second monkey seemed more fitting in a way, since Lewis had been out cheating with girls at his restaurant and Lee would have liked to poison his food just enough to make him sick. But she couldn't do that and get away with it. Tearing up his new store would be another matter. No one knew her in this town, and Lewis, no doubt, had forgotten describing the store to her. True, he wouldn't see the correlation between his behavior and his punishment, at least not right away, but she had observed that if enough things went wrong for people they began to look around in their own lives for things to change. The destruction of his store would be a start.

Tops-N-Things, the store was called. A stupid name, she felt—which typified Lewis. The monkey had cost her three hundred and twenty-five dollars, more than she spent on almost anything but car payments, but if it did what it was supposed to do, she knew in years to come she would count the expense a bargain.

At thirty-seven Lee had a reputation for a fierce moral code, which she cultivated. Actions have consequences, she often said, and she wanted people to remember that. At wakes she was known to glare at people for offenses they'd committed years ago, sometimes against her parents. That, combined with her prematurely gray hair, made her seem like something ancient, a prophet of old. She prided herself on asking the tough questions no one else would and making sure they were answered. Just last year, at the doctor's office, the nurse had come in after the physical and started giving her dietary instructions.

"Why is it," Lee said, erectly balanced on the edge of the chair and buttoning up her blouse, "that I pay for a doctor but end up talking to a nurse?"

"I'm sure I don't know," the nurse said, blushing. She began reordering the brown bottles of hydrogen peroxide on the tabletop and didn't bring up the diet again.

Lee stared at the nurse to let her know her answer was unsatisfactory and felt pleased that this year after her physical the doctor came back to talk to her.

With her students she was strict but fair; helpful to the good ones and a holy terror to those who weren't. If they chewed gum it went on their noses, if they wrote love notes she read the notes aloud, if they didn't do their homework they stayed after school every day for a week. That was how she had learned in Catholic schools and it had served her well. She saw no reason to lower her standards simply because she taught in a public school and people there found her methods harsh. One time her principal had spoken to her about it. His name was Mr. Aubrey, a fat man who had ice cream with all his meals and often, Lee suspected, instead of them. His glasses always seemed vaguely foggy. She sat at her desk and listened to him go on about modern methods—how teachers were so supportive in this day and age and how they needed to nurture students—waiting for him to make his point. He never did, evidently hoping she'd get it herself. When he finished she let the silence hang, staring at him for a full sweep of the second hand on the wall clock, and then told him that modern methods were fine but hers were better. He fiddled with his tie.

"This is a school, not an encounter group," she told him, stacking graded papers, "and students need to respect their teachers, not love them. Mine, you'll recall, always have the highest test scores in the city." He couldn't argue with that and didn't try. She finished tidying her desk and told him the students could get their nurturing at home. He never spoke to her about it again, which was just as well. She had since childhood harbored a secret dislike for fat people, believing them to be in some crucial way morally deficient. If Mr. Aubrey had brought up the subject of right and wrong again he would have tempted her to comment on his eating habits, and that, she knew, would be a mistake.

Sparse fields of corn and cabbage replaced the roadside trees and the heat seemed to worsen, if that was possible. The few people she saw working in the fields wore wide-brimmed straw hats tied on with bright kerchiefs and looked like they were moving in slow motion. Every few hundred feet billboards advertising waterfront restaurants and motels loomed up beside the car and then flipped past, most with seagulls perched on them. She turned up the air-condition-

ing so she and the monkey could ride in comfort. She calculated that she had only a few more miles to go, which made
her happy because the monkey was beginning to smell like
dirty wet wool and because she wanted to get the whole thing
started. She'd been planning it for two weeks and the
prospect of her plans' fruition always filled her with a giddy
excitement. If there hadn't been a monkey in the car she
would have sung. As it was, she permitted herself a quiet,
tuneless hum.

Her sister, Abigail, didn't know what Lee was up to.
They lived together in a small house their parents left them
when they died. Abigail was seven years younger than Lee
and might well have been Lee's child, since Lee spent much
of her own life trying to run Abigail's. She provided this service to anybody, but Abigail, being closest to her, was its pri-
mary beneficiary. Abigail had been dating Lewis for three
years and talked vaguely about marrying him, but never with
any real enthusiasm. Lee thought Lewis was beneath Abigail
and told her so often, but that seemed to have the opposite
of the desired effect so she finally made a promise to herself
not to say anything. It took enormous self-control but the
effort was worthwhile, since it appeared to work. Abigail
stopped bringing Lewis around as much and didn't call him
if he hadn't called for a week and didn't mention his name
at every opportunity. But then Abigail found out Lewis had
been two-timing her and instead of being angry she felt
guilty, as if she'd driven him away by always putting him off
when he said they should marry. For days, she moped around
the house in her bathrobe. Lee couldn't stand to see Abigail
act like that, especially after she'd been wronged, and even

more, she couldn't stand to see Lewis get away with it. She decided to make sure he didn't.

She found that glowering to discomfort him when he came over only caused Lewis to smile, and if she silently rebuked him by her furious presence he merely asked if she had laryngitis. She realized she'd have to do something different but for a long time wasn't sure what. Finally she determined to take some kind of action, since that seemed to be the only thing he respected, and one day, sitting at a table by herself in the teachers' lunchroom, she overheard Miss Sims telling Mrs. Pant that her sister had just bought her niece a monkey and regretted it ever since. The monkey had torn down every one of her draperies the first fifteen minutes in the house.

Lee forced herself to finish her lunch to hide her excitement. She thought Miss Sims' sister was a simpleton—any fool could see that monkeys were no kind of pet—but she was glad she had overheard the two talking. Useless as pets, monkeys could be put to other purposes, and the idea of one serving as the arm of her vengeance pleased her to no end, especially since she had always found Lewis' features vaguely apelike. That very night when she got home she began making discreet calls to pet stores about where she could get a monkey and how much it would cost.

This morning, before leaving for school, she'd told Abigail that she wouldn't be home for dinner. She had a conference to attend after work. Since Abigail didn't like to cook, Lee told her to get some take-out, recommending Chinese over Italian because it was less fattening. She put a menu from the Peking Duck on the kitchen table and circled a few items they usually got in red, having no doubts that Abigail would forget what she'd told her, never being one to pay much attention to things in the morning.

Lee decided to discuss that as well. She said to Abigail, "Are you this oblivious at work in the mornings, too?"

Abigail lowered the paper and scratched her shoulder, visible through a rip in her nightshirt. She said, "I try not to snore when I'm sleeping there."

"You needn't be rude," Lee said, ratcheting her chin a notch higher. "I'm only concerned about your welfare."

The roadside fields gave way to scrubby dunes and here and there rivulets of sand drifted across the pavement. Where the road rose over the dunes Lee caught glimpses of the sea, miles of blue-green swells topped with whitecaps like little dots of whipped cream, and had she not been on so important a mission she would have liked to stop and savor the view. She told herself there would be plenty of time for that later, however, and settled for cracking open her window to let in the smell of the salt air, all the while keeping her eyes peeled for the shop. The monkey, holding a rubber banana with both of its small hands and gnawing on the end, didn't seem to notice any change in its surroundings.

"Wake up," Lee said, rattling the cage. "We've got some business to attend to." The monkey bared its teeth and went on chewing the banana.

At a strip mall, about a half mile from the beach, she found the store—the kind of place that would be crowded on rainy days with small children, whiny because they couldn't go out. Today, with the sun hot enough to melt tar and the sky a clear blue except for a milky haze ringing the horizon, no one would get in her way. She planned to let the monkey go, stay just long enough to ensure that it was doing what she wanted, and then get in her car and leave. A few miles up the road she'd pull over and clean off her license plate, so no one would be suspicious and stop her.

She'd checked to be sure the town had veterinarians. She imagined they would dart the monkey and not shoot it, and then turn it over to a zoo. She had the numbers of two of them memorized, and three quarters in her pocket so that when she was done washing off the license plate she could call one and tell him a wild monkey had gone on a rampage in a store and couldn't he get over there right away and tranquilize it. If he didn't believe her he could phone the store and ask. Even if they traced the monkey to Charlotte they wouldn't catch her—she'd paid cash for it and left without filling out the required forms. All in all, she didn't see what could go wrong.

Just before going into the store she took the key from her purse and unlocked the cage. The monkey watched her suspiciously from the corner, as if distrusting her motives, then reached one hand gingerly forward and pulled on the lock. Lee swatted the hand away so the monkey wouldn't leap out prematurely and, keeping a firm grip on the latch, stepped out of the car, hiding the cage behind an oversized shopping bag. The monkey hooted once as the cage swung free, then stood still, stunned by the heat. The burning pavement scorched Lee's feet. She felt like a snail crossing a hot griddle. The monkey didn't move, but its restless eyes skipped from item to item in the store window.

Inside, Lee shivered. Not from the air-conditioning,

which was pleasant after the blast of heat, but as if being in
the store itself offended her. "Mostly 'Things,' " she sniffed
disapprovingly, looking around the shop. Racks of shirts and
sweaters covered one wall, but the rest was filled with junk:
blown up and lacquered blowfish hanging from the ceiling,
baskets of shells and shell-shaped soaps, sharks' teeth sold
singly or still set in their yawning jaws, cheap sunglasses,
plastic pail and shovel sets, bags of potpourri whose wretched
scent stung her nose. She didn't see anything she would have
bought for herself let alone for anyone else, which figured,
given the shop's owner. Had it been otherwise she would
have been surprised.

"What's that?" the clerk said. He was a fat blond teenager
with steel-rimmed glasses that made his eyes look small and
red, and a particularly unpleasant porcine face. He put down
a model airplane he'd been studying and smiled at her from
behind the counter. There were clusters of pimples on his
cheeks and he had a fat chin and a round nose, and he looked
the way she always imagined some of her least favorite students growing up to look. Good, she thought. That would
make this all the easier.

The monkey gave a high-pitched squeal and rocked the
cage on its handle. The boy, whose name, Johnny Arnold,
was printed on a badge pinned to his chest and who couldn't
see the cage behind the bag, blushed and looked away as if
Lee had burped.

"Tops-N-Things," Lee said, walking up to the counter.
When Johnny looked at her she smiled. "What a pretty name
for a store." She made an unconscious gesture with her hands
as if she were taking off a pair of gloves.

Johnny rubbed his palms together and smiled back. "People sure think so." He seemed to be making an effort to be cheerful.

"Oh?" Lee questioned. "Do a lot of customers comment on it?"

"Not customers, ma'am. Shop people. Three other stores have taken the name up and down the pike since we opened."

She looked at him, a vague warning beginning to make itself heard in the back of her mind like a horn sounding distantly, meant for her. She tried to ignore it but couldn't.

"Surely your boss must get angry," she said, pressing down on the cage's lid. "Can't he bring suit?"

"I suppose, but it's not worth the money."

"And how long has the shop been here?"

"Six months," Johnny said, nodding. He gripped his bangs between his thumb and forefinger and switched them from one side of his forehead to the other. "Well, six months next week. It's been slow going, but we expect business to pick up real soon. Anything you want at all, just tell me and I'll get it for you." He spread his arms out to indicate the whole store. "If it's too big to carry we'll ship at no charge."

Johnny's responses relieved Lee. The owner was a man and the store had been open six months—that meant it had to be Lewis'. He'd come over to their table one night in the winter and bragged about the shop during the entire meal. He could sell more junk to fools there in an hour, he said, than he could all night in a restaurant. He'd toasted himself and his new venture four times.

Lee set the cage down unobtrusively and stepped away from it, examining a rack of belts.

"Those are nice belts," Johnny said, sliding his belly along the counter to be across from her. "I wear them myself."

"Yes." Lee turned one over. The stitching was cheap. She slid her thumbnail into the seam and easily pulled apart the two pieces of fake leather. "I would have thought so."

"You could buy a couple, maybe give some to your friends."

The monkey flipped the cage lid open with a slight bang. Johnny looked at the door to see if someone else was coming in, then back at Lee with a shrug. The monkey shrank down in its cage before standing up and turning completely around, very slowly. Finally it stuck first one leg over the rim and then the other. Lee wanted to make sure the boy didn't see it until it was too late.

"How about those?" she said, nodding at a set of different-sized white T-shirts tacked to the wall above the register. They had the store's name embossed in blue over the silhouette of a jet fighter.

"Those are five ninety-five each," Johnny said. When he looked up at them three rolls of fat bulged over his collar. "They're some of our best-sellers. I designed them myself." He pointed to a rack behind Lee and said, "We've got a whole bunch of them right over there by that—" He stopped in midsentence as if struck dumb, his Adam's apple working up and down. "Monkey," he said finally.

Lee turned to look. The monkey picked up one of the T-shirts and stuck its head through an armhole and pirouetted, hooting. Then it trapped the shirt underfoot and ripped it in half.

"Hey!" Johnny said, waving at the monkey as if that would stop it.

Lee smiled at the boy. "It's got a personality just like your boss's, don't you think?"

Johnny looked at her as if she'd suddenly spoken another language. "My boss? How do you know my grandmother?"

"Your grandmother?" Lee gripped the counter. "Is she the manager?"

"I'm the manager," the boy said, edging around the counter so as not to startle the monkey. Lee could see he meant to catch it. "She's the owner."

"But the owner's a man! You said so." Lee sounded angry, as if she were accusing Johnny of lying, but her whole body seemed to shrink like a house settling into its foundation.

"No I didn't. I didn't say she was anything." Johnny leaned over and ripped a box of shirts from the monkey's hands. "But since you asked, she's my boss and the owner of this store." He grabbed at the monkey, but it skittered away. "She's been waiting fifteen years to open one, and now that I'm old enough to help her she finally has."

The monkey slapped a glass shelf, making the porcelain figurines on it bounce onto the floor, where they shattered on the linoleum.

"Who the hell put this monkey in here?"

"I didn't know your boss was a lady," Lee said, feeling faint. She searched for a chair.

"You!" he said, turning on her. His face was an unhealthy shade of red, midway between a ripe tomato and rotten meat. "This is your monkey?"

The monkey climbed up a step ladder leaning against a

wall and shimmied along a water pipe toward a cluster of brightly colored balloons.

Lee watched his progress. "Mine? No. Well, not really." The monkey reached out to grab the balloons and knocked one of the lacquered blowfish against them. Three balloons popped and the noise sent it somersaulting to the ground, squealing as it fell. "I'm just using it for the day."

The monkey shook its head and grinned up at the balloons, then sauntered toward the back of the store.

"Using it?" Johnny said, following after the monkey. He got within ten feet and threw a beach ball, hoping to scare the monkey into running into the office. The ball caromed off the monkey's shoulders while it was busy contemplating a mannequin. "Using it for what?"

The monkey flipped the mannequin on her back and yanked off one of her legs, which it began swinging over its head like a club. The boy ducked, and the leg cracked open a line of piggy banks, then knocked over a display of Wiffle balls, which bounced away over the floor.

"Don't you have a banana in the back you can give it?" Lee said, stepping toward the boy with her hand out as if to stop him. "It might like that. Maybe it's hungry."

"Oh sure." Huffing, Johnny chased the monkey between a line of shelves. "I keep all kinds of food around in case wild animals come in and start tearing up the place." The monkey seemed to enjoy the chase and tipped over a plastic rack of sunglasses, tripping Johnny. "Bananas for monkeys, steaks for jackals, lettuce in case it's a zebra," he said, on his back on the floor.

The monkey circled the store three times, each time paus-

ing at different places to let the boy get close, tossing flip-
flops and shirts and Frisbees into the air as it went. Lee could
see them at the ends of various aisles, the small monkey
swinging forward on its knuckles, the boy clutching his side
and muttering curses as he ran. Then the monkey leaped up
onto the cash register and squatted on top, scratching its chin.
The boy didn't seem to want to startle it there, and besides,
he was obviously tired. He watched the monkey from across
the store, his head halfway lowered and his hands on his
knees to get his breath, which sounded heavy as a bellows in
his chest. When he stood up again his forehead was shiny with
sweat and dark stains were visible under both arms. He
picked up a fishing pole and moved slowly toward the monkey, trying to prod it into the corner. The monkey chattered
at him and climbed halfway up a light cord.

"Well you must have something that will cover it," Lee
said, looking around a bit dazed at the destruction. "Insurance."

The boy dropped the pole and slapped his forehead.
"Christ! My grandmother's going to kill me. Just last week
an Allstate agent tried to sell me insurance for a monkey rampage and I turned him down." He lunged at the monkey,
who'd eaten the top off a straw boater, but the monkey was
too fast. It scrambled the rest of the way up the light cord
and swung from the lamp, hooting and showing its teeth at
the boy. When the boy jumped up and tried to grab its leg,
the monkey let the boater rim float down on him.

"No, I meant acts of God, that sort of thing," Lee said.

"You're not God, lady," the boy said, squeezing his side
and wincing as he breathed. For the first time he looked like

he might hit her, and she took a step backward, raising her purse protectively, almost to her chin. "But I'd like to know just who you are."

The question stumped her. She reached behind her for a stool and collapsed onto it with an audible thud. "My sister's sister," she wanted to answer, but realized it wouldn't make sense and was no longer appropriate. She looked at the monkey, swinging upside down from the lamp, holding on with its hind legs and snatching at kites stapled to the wall. "The monkey lady," she said finally, but wasn't sure at first what she meant.

"The monkey lady. Great." The boy squatted, then sat on the floor, his legs straight out before him. He watched the monkey rip one of the kites' struts free and nibble at the end as if it were a shrimp. "So you go around and do this everywhere."

"No," Lee said, pulling a shredded shirt from over her shoulder and dropping it to the ground. "With the monkey, just here."

"Oh? And it just happened to be my lucky day?"

"No," she said. She noticed that her hair was out of place, some of it hanging over her forehead, and tried to smooth it back. When it fell across her eyes again she gave up. "A mistake. It's all been a big mistake."

"A mistake!" The boy jumped to his feet and stood over her. "You call this a mistake!" He gesticulated around the room, pointing at the torn kites and ripped clothes and twisted displays littering the floor, the ruined racks, the tattered walls. "You wreck my life and call it a mistake?"

He picked Lee up and shook her. "Lady, my whole life I

wanted nothing more than to grow up and be a fighter pilot but I ended up flat-footed and obese and so nearsighted I can't distinguish my own face in the mirror in the mornings, but last week I got up the nerve to go to the recruiters and see if maybe there wasn't some way around those things and when I came through the door the recruiter laughed and asked me if I wasn't lost." Johnny held her at arm's length, his chest heaving, and turned his head to cough. "I told him what I wanted and he laughed again, this time so hard he fell out of his chair, and when I left the office he was still laughing, sitting there on the floor holding his stomach. So all week I've been stewed off about it, thinking that no, I'm not going to be a fighter pilot and no, no girl's ever going to look at me as something special and in fact they might even laugh at me because I work in my grandmother's shop selling junk. Junk." He looked at the junk scattered about by the monkey. "But I'm coming around, okay? I'm getting used to the idea. I'm telling myself to count my blessings because I've got a grandmother who cares about me and sets me up with a job and then you come along with this monkey and destroy the place, so now I'm not going to work here because there's nothing to work in. I don't know what I'm going to do instead, maybe get a job as a fat-boy bagger in some grocery store where I can't even order model fighter planes to put on the shelves. Fair enough. I can probably handle that too. But I also got to tell my grandmother, who is seventy-six and not very healthy, that her shop is history, and I'm *not* going to tell her it's because some fruitcake came in here with a monkey and made a mistake. You'll have to do better than that."

"You poor boy," Lee said, nearly reaching out and touching him. The boy plunked her down on the stool again and then steadied her, as if she might topple over. She composed her hands on her purse in her lap, surveyed the damage, and sighed. "It's not a mistake, but I don't know what else to call it. I'm at a loss for words."

The boy stood over her, breathing heavily, waiting for her to go on.

The monkey batted a shell wind-chime and the shells clicked together in the silence. Lee watched the shells spin around each other in their wobbly orbits and then turned to Johnny. His eyes seemed huge now behind his glasses, as if they could see everything about her, her whole past in all its petty details. She said, "I made a wrong turn a long time ago, and only now discovered it."

Upside down, holding a blowfish by its tail, the monkey turned its head when Lee spoke, listening. It contemplated her, then hopped down from the ceiling and looked around the store, as if searching for something else to destroy. It tossed the blowfish aside and, seemingly bored, walked to the door and pushed it open and stood on the hot sunny sidewalk, picking up first one foot and then the other, getting its bearings. Finally it lit out straight for the road, making two honking cars swerve to avoid it, and over the dunes toward the sea. Standing side by side, Lee and Johnny could see its head and shoulders as it ambled along the sandy ridge, then just its head with the round flat ears, then nothing but the blue sky and the sand.

THIEF

— ·— ·— ·— ·— ·— ·— ·—

I came out of the butcher's carrying blood sausage and pork chops in one plastic bag, ground beef in another, happy that my Portuguese was at last coming around. For the first time in a shop I'd known the words for everything and hadn't mumbled or stuttered, and the other customers hadn't sighed or smiled patiently while I spoke, encouraging me like a slow child. I bought the ground beef in celebration. It was expensive, more than I could afford, but I was beginning to feel as if I belonged.

I scraped sawdust from my shoes on the edge of the step and smelled chestnuts warming on a brazier. A one-armed man sold them from a donkey cart on the corner every afternoon, ringing a bell to announce his presence, and I'd just decided to buy some when I noticed a woman leaning against the wall, hugging herself, her dark eyes fixed on me. Acne scars pocked her face and her knuckles were huge. She smiled and nodded and I realized she'd been waiting for me, but I couldn't place her. Well, this was another good sign: people knew who I was and wanted to talk. I smiled back and she called me a thief.

At first I didn't understand, because she was still smiling, and because of her accent. I'd been in the country long enough to know she wasn't from Lisbon. She was from the mountains in the north where they lisped the ends of their words and the intonation was closer to Spanish. When I realized she was serious I straightened up and told her there must be some mistake.

"No mistake, sir. Please, come with me."

I followed her across the street and recognized her as the woman who ran a small grocery store on the corner. I'd stopped there before going to the butcher's.

A crowd had gathered outside her store, five or six older men and women, the men in their suits, hats on, the women dressed for shopping, hair dyed blue and curled, plastic bags hanging from their arms. She let me go in first, politely, then crossed the room and stood behind her counter like a judge. Everyone else filed in behind us.

"One of these people saw you take some fruit."

"They couldn't have," I said. "I picked up a few oranges, then put them down before I left."

"I've been watching you," an old lady wearing thick glasses said, nodding her head once for emphasis. "You put them in your bag."

I looked at her and she lifted her handbag with both hands and held it against her chest, protectively.

"That's a lie," I said, forgetting how to say, "That's not true." The woman gasped, and two men advanced a step, as if I'd slapped her. "I put them back in the crate there."

I pointed it out, then opened one of my bags. "I have two kilos of oranges here. I bought them down the street."

The men folded their arms across their chests and stared at me, heads tilted back. I knew what they were thinking: if I'd bought some down the street, why had I bothered with hers? The owner put her hands flat on the counter and leaned her weight on them, still watching me, no longer smiling, waiting for me to say something else.

Disconnected words went through my head; I tried to string them together in a coherent sentence but couldn't. "Polite," I finally said. "Polite. Don't you believe me?"

She shook her head no. I felt my face coloring, which I knew she'd take as a sign of guilt.

A policeman walked by and one of the customers stepped outside to whistle for him. He came over, unsnapping the leather flap over his gun when he saw the size of the crowd, and the shopwoman explained what had happened. He turned to me and I relaxed when I saw the crescent-shaped scar under his eye. I knew him. He was the corner cop. He had his shoes shined three times a day and he kidded me about my accent whenever I asked him directions.

"Did you do this?" he said, very slowly, to make sure I understood.

"No."

"Liar!" the old woman with thick glasses said.

"We knew he was a thief," one of her companions said, a

woman with a mustache and slight beard. I recognized her
from the fishmonger's. "Now we know he's a liar, too."

The cop snapped his fingers at her behind his back.

"Listen," I said. "Let's go to the other shop . . . I bought
these . . . She'll tell you . . . She'll remember . . . If I have
more than that, well . . ." I stopped, embarrassed to hear
myself talking like a two-year-old, and looked from face to
face. The people were old and didn't trust me and didn't
know what I was doing in the neighborhood in the first place.
No one smiled or blinked.

"Come on," I said, starting for the door and knocking a
bunch of dried peppers off their hook in my nervousness.
They rustled as they fell.

The cop nodded and we set off, he and I in front, the store
owner right behind, and then a little knot of people—the
customers who'd been in the store and two or three others
we passed along the way. I heard them whispering questions
as they joined us.

"I can't believe this," I said to the cop, hoping he'd tell me
not to worry. He didn't answer and I was afraid he'd taken
it the wrong way. "She just made an honest mistake," I said.
"That's all." He moved a half-step in front of me, like a mar-
shal stepping out to lead a parade.

The storefront awnings snapped in a cold wind. I looked
at the sky. A thin stream of white smoke stretched from a
chimney across low, dark swirling clouds. A dozen or so people hung out their windows watching us move down the
street and shouting questions as we passed, and I lowered my
head, ashamed. Here and there dog shit smeared the cob-

blestone sidewalk. I stepped around it and tried not to stumble, tried not to get flustered, but I was sweating.

What if the woman didn't remember what I'd bought? What if she remembered the wrong amount?

I almost tripped when someone burst out laughing beside me. It was a beggar woman, propped up in a doorway on a bed of blankets, the stump of her left leg resting on a bench. The end of the stump was shaped like the head of a hammerhead shark, shiny with scars.

"So they finally caught you, José? Well, it's about time!" She laughed and laughed, exposing her gums and her one remaining tooth, too large by half, oblong and twisted sideways.

She was on the corner every day, handing out discarded newspapers for change, and I usually gave her whatever coins I had in my pocket. She smiled at everybody she saw, called them by name, and talked to them as they went by. It was a month or so before I realized she didn't know anyone and made up the names from day to day.

"I didn't do it!" I said to her. "It's a mistake!"

She laughed again, and some of the people walking behind me joined in. One of them hooted derisively. "Listen," I said, cupping her chin in my fingers to make her look at me. "I didn't do it." She laughed once more and I shook her, trying to make her stop. The cop tugged my arm to get me moving and didn't let go.

We came to the shop. It was no wider than a closet, with a single bare bulb hanging by a wire from the ceiling and the old woman who ran it knitting on a stool, her white hair done up in a knot, rimless glasses on the end of her nose. She stood up, startled, as we all tried to squeeze through the door. She had a couple of crates each of oranges and green beans, a bin of apples and another of pears, and a burlap bag of potatoes by the door. These last, she'd told me, she sold only to her regular customers, because of rationing. Next week, if I came back, she'd sell me a kilo.

The officer asked if she remembered selling me oranges.

"Certainly." She pressed her hands together in front of her.

He took the bag from me; holding it up like a turkey, he asked her how much I had bought.

"Two kilos."

He put the bag in the scale's tin basket. The needle swung to a little over 2.2 kilos and stopped there, quivering.

"You see!" the woman with thick glasses said, stepping forward and smiling triumphantly. Her eyes were huge behind her lenses. "He's a thief! I saw him put them in his bag. It was me! I was the one."

"Wrong!" I said, pointing at the scale. "That's wrong!"

The cop yanked me toward the door, his fingers digging into my biceps.

"No, he's right," the shopkeeper said, putting her hands up to stop him. "It's two kilos. My scale's a little off. But I'm going to get it fixed, soon!"

"How long has it been like this?" the cop asked.

"Not long." She began turning some of the pears in the bin so their bruises didn't show. "Just a day or so, I think."

He seemed unsure whether or not to believe her. His shoes creaked as he rocked slowly back and forth and he didn't let go of my arm. I held my breath, waiting for him to decide. After the shopkeeper was done rearranging the pears she looked up, smiled briefly, and then began fiddling with the knot in her hair.

"All right," he said, releasing me and pushing his cap back on his head. "Fix it. Today."

I exhaled and rubbed my arm.

On impulse, I opened all my pockets and the bags of ground beef and blood sausage and held them toward the owner of the other shop. She put her hand on the edge of one, paused, then searched through them with her long bony fingers.

I smiled at her when she was done, raised my eyebrows, and said, "Satisfied?"

She snorted, as if I might have hidden them elsewhere.

"Thief," I heard the woman with thick glasses say. Muttering something about my having thrown them under a car, she pushed her way through the crowd with her purse and left. The cop hesitated. He seemed to be watching me from behind a shield. He shook his head as if he were disappointed in me, then turned away. I knew he'd always suspect I'd stolen the oranges.

I watched them until they were all gone and my breathing calmed down. It was almost dark outside and beginning to rain. I could smell it in the shop, and the reflections of headlights flickered on the shiny pavement. The shopkeeper hung the CLOSED sign on the door and stood beside it, elbows cupped in her palms, waiting for me to leave, but I didn't want to go. I felt safe inside. Eventually she shrugged her shoulders, shut the door and pulled the shade, and then went to the back of the shop, where she pierced an apple with cloves and put it atop a coal burning stove to scent the room. She returned to her knitting.

I thanked her, my Portuguese coming back to me, and said I'd return the next week for more oranges and some potatoes.

"No," she said, bending further over the sweater she was making as if she were having trouble seeing the stitches. "I think these will be the last of the potatoes this winter."

I stood above her a full two minutes, listening to the steady click of her knitting needles and watching the back of her wrinkled neck, waiting for her to look up. She never did.

On my way out I slipped a handful of potatoes into my bag.

CLOUDS

I know all about clouds: cumulus, stratus, nimbostratus, cumulonimbus. It doesn't take much water to make most of them. A small summer cumulus a few hundred yards to a side holds no more than twenty-five or thirty gallons of water, not quite enough to fill a bathtub. Years ago, my wife miscarried. I still remember the bright triangle of blood on the back of her nightdress. Fourteen months later she delivered a boy at Rochester General, dead at birth. I never saw him, and we didn't give him a funeral. I never asked, but I believe stillborn babies are simply thrown away, or at least they were then. Afterward, we had two girls, five years apart, but never another boy. The dead one was recompense, I believe, for not wanting that first child.

Once a week I lie out in a farmer's field, beneath a copper beech high up on one of his hills, and classify all the passing

clouds. I know what weather they'll bring, today and tomorrow, how they formed, and where. To do this undis-
turbed I pay the farmer thirty dollars a week, cash. I have for
fifty-five years. My wife's name was Stan. She died fifteen
years ago, and I had her cremated. I told my daughters that
that was what their mother wanted, though it wasn't. I liked
the idea of her smoke and ashes drifting up to the clouds.

Elise, my oldest, wonders about that thirty dollars, and
wants to cut me off from spending it. I know this because I
have heard her whispering to Gwen over the phone. My
memory is going, Elise says, which is true in spots—sometimes I repeat myself—and she feels I must be losing the
money or being fleeced because I have no real expenses,
which is true, too, to a degree. But my hearing is just fine.

The farmer's name is Stillson, like the wrenches. He's
about that skinny, too. He has a dozen years on me and the
only real sign is his neck, which has deteriorated so badly
talking with him is like talking with a turtle; his head always
droops. Not that we talk much. We never have.

I wandered into his field after the miscarriage. I came
home from the hospital and cleaned up the blood on the bathtub and the bathroom floor and went to bed, disoriented
from two days without sleep and still afraid Stan might die.
And I realized, for the first time, that our child—if that's
what it was at five months—was gone. I couldn't say dead
because I hadn't ever thought of him or her as alive, really,
but nonetheless it was gone. This was a sharp knowledge.
Learning it, I felt as if someone had peeled back my skin and
muscle and ribs to grasp and bind my heart.

Lying on the bed, staring into the corner of the room, I

knew I wouldn't sleep, so I got in the car and drove a while, turning right, left, whichever way I felt like or the road seemed to want to go or the car to follow. I went through the city and then beyond it, past miles of infrequent houses and barns and abandoned garages, and eventually ended up by this field, Stillson's, where I left the car and wandered up the hill and fell down exhausted beneath this copper beech, which was impressive even then.

Stillson woke me, prodding my shoulder with a muddy boot. I don't know what he thought—probably that I was drunk, because I was in his field and my car was half on the road, half against his fence, the driver's door open, the engine running. He seemed rather gruff. Coming to, I remembered that I'd watched the clouds for a long time and found them peaceful, found they filled some of the void that opened when I realized our child was gone, and had finally been able to sleep. I told Stillson I'd pay him thirty dollars a week from then on if he'd leave the small field exactly the way it was, and if I could come and lie there whenever I wanted to.

That was a lot of money back then. It still is, I suppose. Stillson, being the quiet type, never asked what it was for. He's taken his money and held up his end of the bargain, and I've just about never missed a week where I don't come and lie here for an hour or two in good weather, and sometimes in bad. Once a year, on the miscarriage's anniversary, I sprinkle a few more of Stan's ashes on the grass.

Perhaps it's the clouds' impermanence I find so comforting. Always changing, they can't hold grudges or bitter memories, and their shapes don't echo the ground they've covered. Even lenticular clouds, the dish-shaped cumulus over mountaintops that appear stationary for hours, are an illusion. Water molecules rise up one side of the mountain, blown by the wind, condense and enter the cloud, displacing other water, which blows down the far side and evaporates. The cloud is always moving, no more stationary than a river flowing through a lake.

I go to Stillson's field in all weathers: rain, heat, snow, fog. Fog, which is just clouds touching the ground, doesn't hold much water, either. Walking one hundred yards through fog, you'll only come in contact with half a glassful. I don't mind lying out in it. Winters I get stiff fast and have to leave, summers chiggers bite me, or ants or mosquitoes or flies. Just last week my doctor ran his fingers over a crescent of bites on my collarbone and told me I ought to have my bed linen changed more often. I got dressed and said I would, and let it go at that, but I maintained the memory of his fingers on my skin for hours, like a burn. No one has touched my chest since Stan died.

My daughter Elise wonders about the grass she finds on my collar from time to time. Stan never did. She may not have seen it, since we always had our laundry done. Elise says that's a waste of money, and she does mine herself, in fits and starts. If she hasn't done it for a month I send it out and when she sees the laundry tags she gets angry. She shows this by not talking to me while she cleans the house. Days I went to the field I told Stan I was golfing, as I did every other day of the week, and my friends lied for me. Of them, only Bitz is still alive, and he's not much good anymore. Last year he stopped me at the club. He'd bought a new hearing aid and said it had changed his life. He could hear things he couldn't when he was twenty. I steadied him by his elbow and looked right at him, a habit I'd acquired in the long years before the hearing aid, and said, "That's good, Bitz."

He checked his wrist and said, "It's three forty-five, since you asked."

With the few other old club members I see we don't talk so much as have an organ review: which ones work, which ones don't, whether we're going to get some replaced. Toward the end of Stan's life she used to check the obituaries every morning before going to play bridge, to see if her game was still on.

She got her name as a baby. Her brother wanted a brother, and thought she'd turn into a boy if he called her Stan. I started calling her that as a joke, and then somehow it became part of our intimate vocabulary, and then our public one. That happened with a few words or phrases over the years, *tinkle, toot,* others. It's funny how that works: you soak up the world like a cloud soaks up water, and you sprinkle little drops of yourself here and there. If someone collected them all, he might be able to tell what you were really like.

You can think of clouds as air movement made visible. On warm summer days, with the sky blue, pure white clouds widely spaced, each cloud represents small, scattered rising air currents. Today the clouds are round like coins. We always had a lot of money. Perhaps that was our downfall. We were used to traveling a lot, and when Stan first told me she was pregnant I thought it would be the end of the lives we'd led. I was selfish.

"What should we do?" she said, sitting across from me at dinner at the Algonquin, in New York, where we liked to travel weekends. A vast expanse of white linen, silver, and Limoges china, palm fronds in hammered brass urns, endless bottles of champagne, a jazz trio discreet and unobtrusive. I remember each of these details now, as if I studied them daily in a photograph. I looked at her, searched her serious face. Her eyes seemed to be pulling back; she seemed a long way from the life we'd lived, and I thought I knew what she wanted me to say. I don't think I wanted to say it, not really, but all these years later I can't tell if that's true or just wishful thinking. I turned over a fork and pressed my fingertip between the tines. "We could fix it," I said. Instantly, my stomach clenched. I wished I'd never spoken. Stan's eyes narrowed, the only sign of her disapproval, the only sign that she'd even heard me, for the band started up right after and we danced as we always had, as if the spotlight were on us and the world were watching. It seemed to be, then. Sometimes, recalling that dance, I think I already felt her distance as I held her, like she'd shrunk within her skin.

I remember that first day Stillson took my money without counting it—he never has, at least in my presence—and broke off a sprig of grass and chewed the sweet end for a minute while looking up at the sky.

"All right," he said. "But don't stay too long." He took the grass from his mouth and pointed it at some wispy cirrus above a range of hills. The sun shining through them made halos. "Those clouds over there mean rain."

That's what interested me, I guess. How he knew. I asked him, and he said, "It's the air's smell, partly, but mostly it's the clouds' shape. Feathery like that means a storm's coming."

It didn't look like it to me: they were only a few threads, miles up, and the rest of the sky was blue. I saw my first sun dogs, looking at them. But in two hours the sky was gray, the ground soaked from the rain.

So I started reading about clouds. I read Joshua Howard's works, the Englishman who first noted cloud differences and recognizable types, and every other book I could get my hands on. I read, I watched, I read some more. Soon I seemed to know as much as anybody about them. Those cirrus Stillson pointed out are always the first heralds of a coming storm, warm air pushing up over cold, expanding into clouds. Bitz and company, covering for me, thought I had a kept woman somewhere. They noticed my devotion. They kidded me about it—not often, but enough to show they were curious and wanted me to tell. I never did.

I have seen pink clouds and blue ones and orange ones, and— near a volcano—pure white clouds rimmed black with ash. I know about wind shear and tornadoes and waterspouts. I've traveled the world to see peculiar clouds: pink bubblelike ones over Borneo Bay, which occur only at the solstices; rainbow clouds above Victoria Falls; the towering thunderheads of Oklahoma. And once, a dark, perfectly round cloud over the sun, encircled by a rainbow. The sun shone through the cloud's center, like the light through an ophthalmologist's scope. This was right here in Stillson's field. But I've never seen anything someone else hasn't seen.

You'd think, as I'm forgetting things these days, I'd forget the money for Stillson, too, but I won't. That's from too long ago. Nearer things elude me, like my glasses. I went to the same optometrist two days in a row and picked out two pairs of glasses, the second so I wouldn't be in trouble if I lost the first, and the bastard sold me all four pairs. Halfway through paying for the third and fourth I remembered buying the first two, and I looked into the little fellow's eyes and saw that he knew, too, and had all along. I was too embarrassed to say anything. He cradled a Styrofoam coffee cup in both hands and he looked into it when he quoted me the price, as if he were reading it from the cup's bottom.

I wrote myself a note: "Next time you need glasses, get them at Optico, 621 East Ave," and pinned it to the wall by the front door. I may not remember why by then, but at least the little runt won't get any more of my money. Stillson's field I can't forget.

My daughters remember other things, especially Elise, who stops by often. Gwen lives out of town, and I see her no more than every few years. Once I told Elise how Stan and I wanted to play bridge at a friend's house when she was three months old. Both the cook and Blossom, our nursemaid, had the day off. We couldn't find a sitter, so we put Elise in a bureau drawer and shut it, leaving it open just a crack for air. She wouldn't have remembered, of course, but I told her anyway, to give her anger some focus.

A gift from a father who was not the best of one. We

weren't taught to be, then. Servants brought up the children. Besides, the only person I ever fully loved was Stan. I have come close with Elise: I stopped drinking years ago because she asked me to, and when she vacations I find myself counting off days on my calendar, awaiting her return. She has been able to make me laugh, times when she's not too full of herself. Stan, I think, wanted a boy too. Maybe one she could raise to stand up to things in a way his father never did.

My father beat me every Saturday morning, and my mother died very young. She had vapors—she drank too much—and spent afternoons making long lists of European royalty and their favorite foods, as if they might stop by for supper. A gold-tipped fountain pen in cobalt-blue ink, that's what she wrote with, and I've never seen more graceful writing in all my life. I used to retrieve the crumpled lists from the trash bin and trace out the perfect curves and angles of her script, and writing letters now, I still sense her presence on my pages. Handwriting aside, hers was a hollow pursuit, to say the least, and I sometimes wonder if I'm not guilty of the same thing.

Losing Stan's presence was bad enough; losing our shared history was worse. Old jokes that no one else understood or thought funny; nicknames we'd given friends; places we'd eaten or made love. The first hotel we stayed in had a beaten copper pot for a sink. The smell of diesel bus fumes in the morning, or the perfume of oranges and apples set to bake on a woodstove, or the tang of gin and tonics on a sunny patio above the sea—all these had precise meanings for us, which lost their significance in this world when she died.

Before she went, I wanted to ask Stan if she remembered what I'd said at the Algonquin all those years before. She didn't bring it up after the miscarriage—all she cared about was getting pregnant again, which we did shortly—or after the stillbirth. At least not immediately. Then a year or two later, in the midst of a terrible fight, which began as a disagreement about new fabric for a wall covering, she said, "Well, if you don't like it, you can just 'fix it,' right?" She was standing across the room from me, furiously scratching the underside of one forearm, turning the skin a glowing red. I hadn't realized words could come out sounding so cold.

She pretended at first not to understand why I was upset. Later, after we had made up and made love, she said she'd done it to hurt me, which she had. She'd been wanting to get back at me for a long time, she explained, her head on my chest, her fingers knotted in my hair. I could smell the walnut oil from her shampoo. We were silent for a while— I saw the crescent moon enter and pass across our window— and when I asked if she would always feel that way she didn't answer: asleep, or feigning it. I listened to her breathing for hours.

I didn't have the courage to bring it up again before she died. What if she did remember, and that was what she would take of me to her grave, the memory of my failure at the one great test in my life? I preferred the illusion of the possibility of hope.

I almost envy Elise. Her husband had no money. She said she hated it, the crying, the yelling about bills, the kids underfoot. She could have used help, like we had. For three years

she didn't read a book, and she felt like a telephone pole covered with creepers, the way the kids always grabbed her. She
could never keep her floors clean. But every Tuesday she has
dinner with her son, who lives a block away from her, fixes
her car, brings her lilacs and tulips, calls her most nights after
work. Her daughter writes twice a week from college. Neither of ours wrote us once in four years. Perhaps I'd feel differently about my children if I'd spent more time with them.
I'm not indifferent to them, though that must be how it
seems. Nor do I hold their coldness against them: they're
paying me back in kind. It's just as well, I suppose. They
don't follow me around, demanding that I account for my
time. I don't want anyone else at Stillson's.

I still dream sometimes in French. Years ago, my father took
me to France for summers, left me with a family in a small
provincial town. No one there spoke any English, not even
in the family I stayed with. Great pink camellias floated in
glass bowls filled with water all through their house, cut from
trees in their garden. I would stand looking up at the flowers' cupped shape through the water. I was five when we
started this, nine when we stopped. The war. The Great
One. I didn't know about clouds then. I wish I had. I might
have noticed a difference between the air over France and
my native sky. Saturday nights, the whole town went to the
cinema. At intermission, everyone filed out into the village
square, the men and boys on one side, the women and girls
on the other. There was a small fountain in between, water
splashing in the dark, the mossy bricks surrounding it damp
and slippery, crickets calling from fragrant rows of wild

mint. We would do our business against the wall, the women
and girls watching, and then we'd all file back in and see the
end of the movie.

Stan got involved in charity golf events. I thought once she
was having an affair, the way Ray encircled her with his
arms, showing her how to swing the club just so, the way
she smiled up at him, leaned back into his chest. A sharp
knowledge, but it didn't last. Ray was the club pro. I thought
about it, thought about following her even, but realized she
didn't have time for an affair. When she said she went to
lunch with her friends, she had to go; they were always at
the club. Bitz's wife was there, too. I would have heard.
Nights she was with me. Movies, parties, the theater, sometimes the symphony. Twice a year we traveled. That's when
I saw those different clouds.

I would read about them in a cloud atlas, study their
forms—drawn, mostly, but photographed more recently—
and decide which ones I wanted to see. I never chose, really,
just let the knowledge come to me. I'd flip through the
pages, not thinking, and something would strike me, a line,
a certain cast of light, and I'd know: these were the clouds
I wanted to see next. I'd look up where they were preva-
lent, and when, and get travel literature for the place, and
convince Stan we should go. Most often that wasn't hard.
Stan liked to travel. We'd visit museums, find good restaurants—duck, veal, skewered lamb rubbed with lemon and
garlic and wrapped in bacon, all of which Stan loved—write
letters to our friends. Stan, I'd say, I've always wanted to go
to Borneo. She never remarked that I hadn't brought up this

burning desire before. Sometimes I wondered if that indi-
cated a lack of attention to what I said, because she didn't
care; other times I hoped it meant she accepted my eccen-
tricities, or loved the idea that she didn't know everything
about me even after fifteen or twenty years of marriage.

Getting to see the thunderheads of Oklahoma I had to
work on. I couldn't say I'd always wanted to go to Oklahoma, and once there, I had to beg her to go up in a plane
with me, to fly right into them. The pilot was no problem.
He doubled his fee. I was scared, secretly, that we wouldn't
come back, and I wanted her with me, just in case. Not for
comfort, but because years before, when we'd first started
flying, we agreed we would always fly together, so that if
something happened neither of us would be left behind. She
didn't seem to remember that then, staring out the window
at the swirling darkness, and I didn't bring it up. I wanted
her to remember it on her own, and I didn't want her to dis-
avow it. Perhaps it was another mooring line she'd cast
adrift.

I remember scenes from all those years at odd times: reading the paper or checking the mail, I suddenly see myself
walking past Lisbon bakeries in the heat of the day, or driving
up the coastal highway under a violet dusk, a full moon rising over a stand of pines, or sitting dockside near some lake,
water lapping, air crisp, a high wind blowing a few crimson
leaves over the water. Sometimes light sets off the memories, sometimes smell. Our children appear in a few, not
many. If I think hard I can often figure out the connections.
Once, turning the soil in our garden, preparing it for bulbs,

I remembered going into a dark, narrow shoe store in Au-
toire with Stan, where the cobbler measured her feet thirteen different ways. We spent an hour sorting through
leather samples. She had six pairs made and mourned the
passing of each one. The scene appeared as vivid as a movie
in my mind, her fingers flipping through the leather, the
smell of the tanned hides. After, I decided it was the light—
a certain dull slant to it through the deep green leaves that
meant it had to be an early fall afternoon. In spring, the
same slanting light would be yellower. That night, after
looking up the trip in one of my journals and discovering that
we had indeed taken it during the fall, I mentioned the memory to Stan. She said that that afternoon, at about the time
I'd been working in the garden, she remembered the same
trip, though a different part. She'd found her pearl earrings
on a windowsill. Picking them up, she saw herself buying
them at L'Auberge, and wearing them that same night for a
dinner in a small restaurant we saw starred in the Michelin
guide a year later. I miss those odd coincidences. Perhaps
there was nothing to them, but they seemed a sign of our
love.

Mostly those years blur together. The country club, trips,
the children in school and then in college, Stillson's field,
books of clouds, Stan filling the house with flowers every
week. She liked pink tulips on the polished black surface of
the piano.

I don't have sharp memories of her physical presence
now, and I can't hear her voice, consciously, though I do in
my dreams, and unless I concentrate I can't make her move.
All the movements she made, all the ones I watched her make

for years: walking, skiing, arching above me, and I can't see any of them in my mind's eye. Only her lips move in the images I conjure up, though silently, and her face, turning away from me.

She was sick for five years at the end, and both of us knew what it meant. Sitting beside her in the last weeks I remembered that years before, one warm summer night soon after we'd moved out of the city, a place I thought had too many bad memories, we were lying in bed and Stan said, "I don't know where I'll go when I die." I said, "Nobody does," and jabbed her shoulder lightly.

"That's not what I mean." She pulled the curtain aside and looked out at the street. Crickets chirped, the pavement glowed yellow in the street light, the heat seemed to settle. Half her face was highlighted. "I mean I have no place to be buried. Everyone else in my family is together but there's no room anymore, and besides, I wouldn't want to be with them." She seemed inconsolable, and her words punctured me. I couldn't speak. We never talked about that toward the end. It's just as well, I suppose. It made cremation easier.

Stillson had a son. He was a quiet boy. I would often see them walking the fields together, Stillson pointing out to him airplanes or the way dust whirled before the wind. When they crossed the fields toward me, Stillson walked with his hand on the boy's shoulder. The boy would never come close. He stood by a fence post, watching, always the same one. There's a dent in it even now I swear his shoulder made. He died in the war. The week Stillson got the news was the only week he didn't come. We'd had six days of nimbostratus

clouds that week, unusual for these parts, and I thought Stillson was worried about too much rain.

The next week, he wouldn't take the money from the
week before.

The fence post is still there. From time to time I see Stillson rub it absently as he passes, as if it might bring him luck.
I wonder if he even knows he's doing it.

Years may go by. I remember you too clearly. I wonder if
Stan didn't, too. I lie back, feel the grass, springy beneath
my shoulders, tickling my neck. There's not a cloud in the
sky, just the blue heavens, arching and empty.

Grass

––·–·–·––·–·–·––·–·––

Poa compressa, Canadian bluegrass, grows well in both damp and dry climates, blooms the entire season, won't brown even with a late frost, and is a real royal blue; in the right sunlight it looks painted. The first crop on my brother Eugene's grave has come in thick, almost plush, and kneeling on it, sliding the outside edge of the grass shear's blade flush with the polished granite headstone, I hear the swift double knock of a woodpecker in a tree and remember Eugene in his youth as sharply as if he stood before me now: a tank top, shorts, dusty shoes. His skin is tanned and cut from falls, from fights, from accidents. His shoulders are muscular; his slicked hair glistens in the sun. Mother stands above him, shaking a lemon over his bent brown head as if to baptize him, scolding him for his latest mischief, and when she drops the lemon, yellow in the grass, Eugene picks it up,

scrapes his thumbnail down its skin, and raises it to his face
to smell. Then he hands the lemon back. Mother straight-
ens, turns away, smiling, rubbing the lemon as she walks.
The incident has already vanished from her mind. Eugene
pulls a book from under his shirt and sits against a tree to
read, the book's red leather binding propped on his knees.
The book is a tale of pirates and their deaths, which he has
stolen from the library. Hours later, near dusk, the mosquitoes swarming, swallows rising through the heavy blue
air, Father finds Eugene still sitting against the tree with the
book. He takes the book from Eugene's hands, marks
the page, lays it aside on the grass, and slaps Eugene across
the face, twice. The slaps echo off the garage, like twinned
distant shots. Eugene has been dismissed from yet another
school—gambling again, on golf. He is twelve years old.

I sit back on my heels and take a small leather notebook
from my pocket to write down this memory, which is one
of the many things I hope to tell Sandra, my great-niece. The
brown notebook is old but unused, and I hear its spine crack
as I smooth open its pages. A few days ago, Sandra called and
asked how I was feeling, if I was still following baseball, how
my garden was coming. I'd taken her to a few games as a
child, collected autographs for her, but that was years ago,
and I knew that the real subject of her call was yet to surface. I believe she is interested in asking some questions
about her relatives, especially my brother—her grandfather—and his wife. At least, this is what I am hoping.

Eugene is not buried next to my parents. He has a plot he
paid for years ago, between his wife's and a tilting box elder.
The neat green rectangle their graves make leaves no room

for other graves, not even for those of their daughters, should they so desire. For years, I thought I would never tend Eugene's grave, though I admired how he withstood those slaps, his imperious refusal to acknowledge them even when the red print of my father's hand lingered on his face for hours because of his fair skin. After Father hit him that time, Eugene picked up the book and began reading again, or pretended to. The light was fading so fast I doubted he could see the page. The swallows, still tumbling and turning like a school of fish, I perceived as a sense of movement in the dark sky, a darting shadow.

Father never hit me, or any of the rest of us. Eugene seemed marked off, as if he and Father had agreed early on that the hitting was in some secret way necessary, though the hitting never seemed to change anything: Eugene was suspended or dismissed from four other schools before finally graduating from St. Martin's and going on to Yale. Father died years before I thought of asking him why he had hit Eugene so often, and Eugene, even at twelve, seemed distant from the family, as if he were watching us all, himself included, from some private remove. Had I asked him, I believe he would have ignored me. That aloofness first attracted and then repelled me—I wanted to be like Eugene; I wanted nothing to do with him. Now, passing my hand over the thick blue grass above his grave, letting the blades tickle my palm, feeling them bend beneath the weight of my slight touch, I am simply happy he was my brother.

Finished with Eugene's grave, I move on to his wife's. The grass is even thicker here, powdery soft. Its roots grow many feet in a season, binding the soil, keeping wind and rain from blowing everything away. Like most grass it has a peculiar, earthy smell, which to me is the smell of death, I've encountered it on so many graves. Their stones are the same clay-colored granite, though Olivia's requires more work to keep clean. A few steps closer to the cemetery road, it collects that much more dust in its carved letters. Rubbing dirt from the letters, I see her name written across my reflection on the polished stone.

I met Eugene's wife a year before he did, at the Chatter Box Club's Christmas Ball. Olivia is a pretty name, but for some reason Eugene always called her Stan, even putting that name on her stone. I was standing by the punch bowl when she entered, and saw the smooth whiteness of her neck and shoulders when a chaperone took her stole, her soft curving profile as she turned away. Her neck reminded me of sculpture, and I had never seen lips so red. I walked by her seat three times, the second and third times waving to an imaginary friend at the far end of the floor to give myself a reason to pass, but I hadn't the nerve to talk to her or even to come close enough to smell her perfume. She sat on the edge of the chair, looking out over that sea of dancers expectantly, her tulle dress spread out at her feet, and I found her beauty unapproachable. She and Eugene were a good match. The notebook I am using was hers, her initials stamped in gold leaf in the upper right-hand corner. I found it in one of Eugene's drawers.

I was an usher at their wedding. For most of it, I stood on the edges of the crowd and stared. They seemed to me like people I read about, otherworldly. Their guest list numbered close to six hundred, and the social editor at the *Democrat and Chronicle* devoted a full page to their reception. I think that's why I asked first Gwen and then Abigail to marry me that next year; I wanted in some way, in many ways, to be like them. I hoped marriage would make me special.

Done for the day, I stand and take a few steps back to inspect my handiwork, the straps of my gardener's kneepads pinching the skin behind my knees. My back is sore and my fingers ache but I can see my work has been worthwhile: Eugene's and Olivia's graves look splendid. Green and trim, they stand out from those around them like islands in this sea of ragged stones, as the two did in life.

Tomorrow, I will work on Abigail's grave, and Mother's and Father's, and then, if the weather holds, earlier generations' later in the week. Abigail, who was once my fiancée, and whose grave is the only one I tend that is not a member of our family.

Driving back through the cemetery, slowly, so as not to raise dust from the rutted dirt track, the trees' shadows moving up over the hood and windshield, I remember Eugene and Olivia's first child, stillborn, and never buried. I think that was the only moment of their lives I wouldn't have lived.

Home again, I place the spade, trowel, gardener's fork, and grass shears on the rubber mat by the door and lean their pitted wooden handles against the wainscoting. Above them, I see a framed picture of Eugene and remember the heat of the day the picture was taken as if the memory existed in my

body and not my mind. I feel drained and heavy, submerged
in a bath of too hot water.

The yellowed picture, with decorative, scalloped edges,
is not a very good one—you can just make out Eugene's face,
and mine in profile, looking at him, both of us nearly over-
whelmed by the jungle growth surrounding us. But I've hung
the picture by the door on purpose. I see it whenever I leave
or enter the house and it reminds me of Eugene's better qualities. I will have to show it to Sandra.

I was a sergeant in the Chemical Warfare Service of the
Army in World War II. Eugene joined the navy and was
named skipper of his own ship, a minesweeper, though before the war he had never served. In fact, his only experi-
ence with boats was on transatlantic crossings. He rose to the
rank of lieutenant commander. I was stationed in Hollandia,
Dutch New Guinea, for ten months, and I never quite understood what my assignment was. It's called Sukarnapura,
Indonesia, now. Mostly I dug ditches, which other people
later came along and filled. Once, in the middle of a hot day,
a day like a blowtorch—and it is the sapping weight of this
heat I remember—I was digging ditches with Fletcher, who
was from MIT and weighed 118 pounds, and Stevens, from
some California school. He stood six and a half feet tall and
his Adam's apple looked like a partially swallowed brick.
Working, we'd stripped to our shorts and T-shirts, the same
color green as the swarming, buzzing flies and the watery
mud sucking at our ankles, and I'd just lowered my head onto
my crossed wrists for a rest when I heard someone whistle
at us, as if we were pretty women.

I looked up and saw Eugene on the berm, all in white, his

brass buttons shining in the sun, the razor grass behind him
waving like wheat in the hot wind. Stevens and Fletcher, seeing the uniform, straightened and saluted, their dog tags tin-
kling, but I couldn't move. Eugene's dead, I thought, and
this was his ghost. I felt the hailstone-size welts the fly bites
left on my shoulders and the warm mud eating at my rotten
feet and my swollen hands squeezing the wooden pick-ax
handle so hard I thought they'd burst. Somehow he'd come
to tell me he was dead, and I didn't blink when sweat stung
my eyes, afraid he'd disappear.

"Good thing they've got you three here," Eugene said,
smiling. "If they put you anywhere else you might lose the
war all by yourselves." He returned the salute and told us
to knock off work for a while, having arranged it with
our CO.

He had wangled leave to come and see me. He'd had a
chance to go home and see Olivia and his daughters—I found
this out later, from one of his friends and superiors—but had
come west instead, further into the combat zone. I believe
he thought I was in much greater danger than I ever was—
though Stevens was later killed by a sniper's bullet as he
wandered along a nearby beach—and wanted to talk with me
again in case something happened.

I have always relished that memory—it overlaid some
earlier, painful ones—and I take the picture from the wall
and study it, searching Eugene's face for clues to what mo-
tivated him, then and always. His inscription—*To Francis,
Penny,* the name his friends always called him—is faded to a
rust color but still legible, and I trace the letters with one

dirty fingernail before rehanging the picture and climbing the narrow stairs for a bath. On the upper landing the sun through the window is still hot and I pause in it, warming myself like a cat, one of the true pleasures of age.

Before bathing I lay out my clothes, and opening the squeaky sock drawer I smell the faint scent of cedar. This is Eugene's bureau, which I took after he died. On the back, scratched in rickety handwriting seventy-five years ago, is my own name. I doubt Eugene ever saw it. Mother always kept bags of cedar chips in our drawers, lavender in hers, and it was that lavender scent which first attracted me to Gwen. She was a brief interlude in my life, but she marks a change for me, the time when Eugene first began to show an almost casual cruelty toward me. This story may pain Sandra, but I believe she should know it, and so, like my other memories, I record it.

I had asked Gwen to marry me. Though far wealthier, she was a pale imitation of Olivia, skin neither as smooth nor as soft, her neck a bit too short, retiring where Olivia was anything but. We had dated for several months. Dances, picnics in brown October fields, skating on our summer house's frozen lake, a chaperoned trip to New York. In a horse-drawn cab there, holding my hand, momentarily free of the chaperone, she had given me reason to hope. Outside, I remember, it was bitter cold; the horses leaned into the drilling wind, mufflers and a turned up collar hid the cabbie's face. A string of gaslights circled the park like a necklace and every few seconds gusts of snow blew across them, spreading their yellow light in the air like a stain. Gwen's fur-framed face shone in the gaslight, lending her small, uneven features a transitory beauty, and the lavender scent of her perfume filled the cab; when I bent to kiss her I thought I had sealed our future.

A month later, standing outside our house on a cold sunny early spring day, I asked Eugene if he knew why she had turned me down. The lake ice was pewter-colored in the sun, charcoal in the shade. Ribbons of fine snow lay across it, like blown sand.

"Don't you know?" he said, lighting a cigarette and narrowing his eyes against the smoke that curled around him.

I shook my head. A blast of wind made us lean closer. His hair had frozen in tufts.

He looked down the long narrow expanse of the lake toward the tree-covered hills on the far end, the afternoon sky above them a pale watery blue. "It's because of the way you are."

He glanced at me briefly, as if awaiting my response, but I didn't have one. I didn't know what he meant. He looked away again over the lake and inhaled deeply on the cigarette, the end of it brightening, blew smoke slowly out his nose.

"You live your life an inch at a time," he said, flicking the cigarette away. We both watched the wind pick it up, send its glowing red end skittering over the bumpy pewter-colored ice. When the glow died out, he said, "She's not like that, and she said it would drive her crazy." He turned to face me, his back to the wind. "Frankly, it would me, too."

Even as a child I had always suspected Eugene disapproved of the care I took with things, but he had never been so ob-

vious. Father traveled: Rome, Prague, Paris, Madrid, then
later Bangkok and Peking. From every city he brought me
coins. Eugene wasn't interested. Once he accompanied me
on the downtown trolley to Sibley's and waited patiently
while I chose among several display cases, settling finally on
a mahogany frame with etched glass and gold corner seals.
When I thanked Eugene he dismissed the notion, saying he'd
done it only because Father had said he would give him an
extra two dollars for the trip, and planned to buy cigars and
a new shirt with the money, which he did. But he carried the
case home for me, and a year later, when he ran into my
room to tell me one of the cooks had started a fire in the
kitchen that threatened the house, he grabbed the case and
carried it out onto the lawn.

The fire never spread, but in gratitude I spent the next
morning cleaning all the coins with a silver polish that
smelled like ink, memorizing their locations and descriptions
so I could impress Eugene with my knowledge. He accepted
the collection, ran off with it tucked carelessly under his arm,
and traded it for two peppermint ice cream sodas, neither
of which was for me. Still, these things were hard to read;
for every seemingly cruel or thoughtless act there was another equally generous one. After Gwen, Eugene's actions
became more sharply defined.

Less than a year after Gwen, I was engaged. Abigail was
a sweet girl. My friends all envied me, though Eugene didn't
seem to approve. He told me he and Stan wouldn't make it
back from their Brazilian trip for the wedding, but that both
of them knew it would be a fine affair. Two months before
the wedding, there was an accident. I was driving. Abigail

was only twenty-four when she died. All these years later, I still tend her grave.

Sitting by my open window and watching the blue sky turn violet, I hear children shouting in the street and the burring sound of mowers as a few late-working fathers cut their lawns. The phone has not rung tonight, as I hoped it would, which has left me feeling the slight, dry scratch of disappointment. Looking at my desk I see Olivia's open brown notebook and the disappointment turns into the sudden burn of shame. I often felt that way around Eugene, times he denied me. But then I tell myself to have faith, to wait, that Sandra will call, that I have not misjudged her.

I have taken a hot bath and completed my regimen of stretching and rubbing eucalyptus liniment into my shoulders, arms, and legs. Never especially limber—and therefore never much of an athlete—if I fail to do this nights after working on the graves, I sleep fitfully and awake the next day stiff, barely able to move. Now and then a breeze blows through my curtains and cools my damp chest, bringing with it the smell of the cut grass, and when the breeze is still the eucalyptus liniment clears my sinuses. A sort of cosmic breathing in and out, the smells of age and death.

At the end of his life, I kept much the same regimen for Eugene. He could not bend enough to reach his feet and care for them. Each night I rubbed a Dixie cup of ice over his heels to relieve his swelling, and in the mornings, after he bathed, I worked the eucalyptus liniment into his heels and ankles to loosen them. His feet were dry, rough, very light—almost as light as the feet of a child—but the oranged, horned skin

gave them away. In places, it bubbled away from the muscle like the skin of a grilled chicken. I worked fifteen minutes on each foot. I would wake him with a phone call and
by the time I arrived he'd have finished bathing; at night, I
stopped by about nine and would find him dressed for bed.
We rarely spoke, but I believe he appreciated my care. I
moved his bed closer to the window, as he said he liked to
watch the night sky.

It is an unusually warm night, in the seventies though it
is now ten o'clock, but you still know it's spring. Even with
the windows open, the night is quiet. A month from now,
it will pulse with the songs of crickets. I remember watching Eugene shimmy down the drainpipe from these same
third-floor windows summer nights, on his way to meet
girls or friends or just to find adventure. I would hang out
the window, the sill cutting into my stomach, and he would
call to me, standing a white blur in the dark, dusting his hands
on his trousers, urging me to come along. The scent of ma-
nure from Mother's garden and the chirping of cicadas filled
the night air, and though I wanted to, I could never bring myself to join him.

One summer—my tenth, Eugene's thirteenth—I finally
joined in on some of Eugene's mischief. It started as a way
to save money: on weekends, we would walk the seven
miles from our house to the farm instead of taking the morning trolley, saying we had caught a later one. Soon the walks
came to be about more than money—they were about pleasure, a mutual pleasure in the physical world. The wheat-
and cornfields lining the road crackled in the summer heat
or rustled in the wind with a sound like rain, and the sun re-

flecting off the pavement baked our cheekbones. Dust covered the ground, so thick sometimes it was choking, rising
to turn our black shoes white, and we walked through it quietly for long hours, only our footsteps on the macadam making noise. We would both look up at the sudden shadow of
a passing cloud or the silent flight of distant birds, and when
we heard cars coming from a long way off we stood on the
roadside and tried to guess what make and model they would
be from the pitch of their engines. Eugene suggested we
wager on our guesses. Most times he won my carfare. Toward the end of that summer, I had started to call him Penny.

All this we both liked without ever having to say so. I liked
being with Eugene, equals for once, just the two of us on the
road, searching for snakes and frogs and dropped treasures
from cars. Occasionally, when we tired or saw storms moving toward us over the hills, we hitched a ride, but more
often we walked through the rain, enjoying the steam rising
from the pavement when the first drops hit and our clinging
clothes and the streams beneath the bridges swelling and
foaming in the sudden downpours.

Our walks came to an abrupt end in August, when Father
found out what we were up to. I'm still not quite sure how.
One humid morning Father pulled me into his office by my
ear. Heavy curtains shut out the light and in the darkness I
stumbled over an ottoman, but even as I fell Father didn't
release his grip so that for a few seconds I seemed to be
swinging in space by my ear. I gasped at the pain.

Father let go and stood over me where I'd fallen on the
rug. "Your brother made you do this."

"No," I said, rubbing my ear. I knew what he was talking

about but for a moment I couldn't say anything, rocking on
my knees to quiet the pain. Father never liked us to show
we felt things. "It wasn't like that at all. It was his idea, but
I wanted to. I'll repay all the money. We didn't do it for
that." I stood, cupping my ear. It was circled by a ring of pain,
like fire, and the ring was pulsing. "I wanted to."

"How much money?" he said.

"I don't know. I haven't kept track. Fares out to the farm
every week. It's really not that much. I can repay you in a
month."

He didn't answer. He moved to his desk and pushed a glass
ink bottle in and out of the desk lamp's circle of light, slowly,
the blue liquid sloshing up the bottle sides and leaving pale
blue stains as it receded. This was his way when he was lost
in thought, occupying his hands and ignoring whoever else
was in the room.

Later, I sat on the curb, marking it with a hunk of chalk.
Eugene came out, his face red and glowing. The skin looked
as if it had been exposed to the sun for too long and then had
four strips peeled off. Those were the marks from Father's
hand. I had heard some of the slaps over the lawn.

"Penny," I said, reaching for his arm. He pulled away and
I chased after him.

"Penny! What happened?"

Suddenly I was facedown on the ground and Eugene was
astride my back, pushing my face in the dirt.

"You know what happened, you bastard. You told him."
He kicked my legs with his heels.

Arching my neck to get my mouth out of the dirt, I said,
"I didn't. I swear."

"Did you tell him about the money?"

"Yes, but he knew."

He slammed my head down again. "Father said you told him everything." Eugene punched me once and got off. The red on his face had intensified. Though I ran beside him, the chalk still gripped in my hand, he refused to listen to anything I said. He had learned that trait well from Father.

Lying in bed, my ear still sore, I realized there was the slightest chance that Eugene was right, that Father had pulled me in to his office to talk about something else—swimming in the lake with no adult supervision, which he had strictly forbidden and which we had begun to do the week before—and that I'd blurted out news of our walks prematurely. I didn't think anyone had seen us, but I would never know, of course, because if I asked Father I might get us in trouble for something else and he would ignore the question anyway. As for Eugene, he would always be sure of my betrayal.

Those roads we walked are gone now. Widened, abandoned, developed: I couldn't walk them if I chose to—they exist only in my memory. Once, after Eugene died, I started to drive out to find them. On the way, after passing the first familiar building—a partially collapsed but still recognizable barn—I realized that too much had changed and if I drove the roads I would be driving them through my memories, changing them forever, and losing them as I had lost Eugene. I turned back without regrets.

For the rest of that tenth summer, and for all the summers until we learned to drive, Father had us driven out to the farm. He made us repay a summer's worth of trolley fares and it wiped out my savings. Eugene had none, but getting money was easy for him: he played three rounds of golf with older men and won twice what he needed.

And, sure that I'd turned on him, Eugene distanced himself from me every chance he got. Soon enough he was off on other schemes with older friends, stealing grapes from Wylie's vineyard, swimming in the nearby abandoned quarries and canals, watching the servant girls take tub baths in their quarters, but I still wish those walks had never ended. Losing them was bitter then, and seems so even now.

On some of those nights I went to Eugene, one of his feet cupped in my palm, I was tempted to tell him, "Eugene, you were wrong about me. I never betrayed us. Father already knew." But I didn't. Eugene should never have said all the things he said to me, because he was my brother, and because he was my brother I did not tell him he had been wrong. It would have served only to bring regret into his life at a time when he could do little to assuage it. For so long, he had been the protagonist in my life and I just his shadow, and now it was my turn to shoulder some of the burden. So I held my tongue and worked on his painful feet until it was almost dark, and he was asleep or resting.

The sweet scent of vanilla grass, *Hierochloe odorata,* fills the air. The cemetery is quiet this morning—some birds, a squirrel chattering at my presence, the distant rumble of a jet. The early yellow sunlight slants onto the grave stones through the trees, shifting over them with the wind. I sit in the car a few moments, the door open, my shoes on the brick roadbed, and let the smell of the vanilla grass fill my lungs. Sandra will like this smell, I believe; it's sweeter than perfume.

Nine months of the year I keep a small portable mower in my trunk. Novembers I bring it into my basement, wash the housing, drain the fluids, and disassemble the engine parts, soaking them in oil to loosen the grime and dirt before drying and reassembling them. I discard the spark plug and oil filter and wrap the motor in a sheet to keep it dust-free, then reverse the process in the middle of each March. One year I catalogued forty-three different types of grasses in the grit, including a seed of the inaptly named meadow oat grass, *Arrhenatherum elatius,* which flourishes along the edges of deserts in the Southwest. I thought perhaps it had come this far north caught in the feathers of a migrating goose. Like all meadow oat seeds, it had a twisted awn protruding from its back that untwists and drives the seed beneath the soil when it rains. I moistened my palm and watched the seed try to bury itself in my skin.

Though the mower weighs only thirty-seven pounds I can feel it growing heavier each year. I have perhaps two or three more summers when I can use it, and now, before assembling the handle, I look over Abigail's grave. Last week, what had been a cold spring gave way to ninety-degree heat in mid-May, and the magnolia blossoms have come and gone. They are so thick on the ground I have the momentarily disconcerting impression that it has snowed on Abigail's grave, and hers alone, or that her grave has been covered in lime. Cholera victims used to be marked off that way. At nighttime in this cemetery, I have read, ranks of their graves fairly glowed.

I walk to her grave and scoop up a handful of the silky magnolia petals, rub them between my fingers. Graves have their own lives, much like those of people. A bright birth attended with great fanfare, a long stretch of slowly decreasing attention, spans of forgetfulness, finally abandonment. Abigail's grave, like her life, moved through these phases more quickly than most.

She was her parents' youngest child, and their favorite. They were not from here, and they bought a creekside plot—not an especially advantageous site—in a small dell in the cemetery. It isn't easily reached, and wasn't then. I think they wanted to forget that she had died, not to forget her, but the practical results were the same. They stopped visiting before long and, as Abigail died before she was an aunt to nieces and nephews, none of them looked after her grave as they grew older.

It is not a particularly prepossessing place even now. Her parents planted the magnolia too near it, and it has never grown to any great height, so its low branches give too much shade, and the covering vanilla grass is thin, even patchy. Still, I like it here. This grass blooms far earlier than other grasses and almost no one ever sees it flower, which is somehow fitting. The grass has other qualities, as well, though I admit I didn't recognize them at first myself. It grows in swampy places and in wet meadows and is the sweetest smelling of all grasses. In the South, Creoles make fans from it, and western Indians burned it ceremoniously. Nearer to home the local Indians used to weave the whole plant into screens, then dampen the screens and place them in a breeze to perfume the air. Even now, in northern European farming villages, villagers scatter vanilla grass before the churches on saints' days and holy festivals to make the pathways leading to saints' shrines fragrant. There, they call it holy grass.

I have a busy morning, clearing vines from Abigail's stone and applying a fertilizer mix to the yellowed grass, phosphates to thicken it, nitrogen to make it green. A year after Abigail died, I was sitting at the end of our dock at night. The noise and smoke of Eugene and Olivia's house party had made me claustrophobic, so I'd wandered outside to get some fresh air. After a few minutes, when I'd begun to forget the noise coming from the house and could hear behind it the quite voice of the summer night—waves and crickets and rubbing branches on the shore—I heard footsteps thumping down the long dock toward me. Drunken, I guessed, from the way they hurried and stopped, wobbled, then went on, and soon enough Eugene called out to me, and when I turned he was waving a bottle and grinning.

"Morose," he shouted. His voice echoed off the ring of trees surrounding the lake.

I didn't answer, and he waited until he was right beside me and said, "Why are you always so morose these days?"

I looked back over the water. A car was making its slow way down West Lake Road, and I watched its lights funneling through the darkness. Eugene fell into one of the Adirondack chairs beside me.

"Is it that damn Abigail thing?" He leaned closer to me, his white teeth flashing, and I could smell the gin on his breath. "Don't be stupid." He held out the bottle and I shook my head, so he swigged from the bottle, emptying it, and threw it on the water, in front of where I sat. "You're better off the way you are, you know. I mean, she was all right, if what you wanted was a life without much pleasure and a lot of boredom."

He was still punishing me for something that hadn't ever happened, all those years earlier, but because I still had that sliver of doubt about my own complicity in what he saw as my betrayal, I sat there and took it. I watched the bottle bob away, ghostly white on the dark water, and wished he would leave. Eugene tapped his foot on the dock, keeping time with an up-tempo song the band had begun to play, and let his head loll back against the chair. I could feel his tapping reverberate up my spine. "Lots of stars," he said, looking up at the sky, and it was true, there were. The Milky Way arched above us like a vast dust cloud. "Thousands of them. Might make you believe in God."

He leaned toward me again. "You do believe, don't you? I mean, I know I've had my doubts. In fact, I never believed in God until you had that accident." He sat back. "It was the best thing that ever happened to you. She was a—" I dumped him into the lake, chair and all, before he could finish, one of the few times in my life I've acted precipitously, and I have never regretted it. It was years before that comment ceased to burn, and even now, when I'm at the club and hear someone drunk in the summer or the smell of spilled gin at the bar tickles my nose, I find it hasn't completely healed.

Before gathering my tools, I look at the leather notebook, open in my palm, two creamy yellowed pages untouched as yet by ink, and decide not to write down this story. It is perhaps better left unknown.

For lunch I sit against a tree with a cheese sandwich and a thermos of iced coffee, Mother's favorite meal. High white cumulus drift across the blue sky and reeds rattle over the stream in a warm breeze, shaking their flat seeds on the water. They will float downstream and embed themselves in banks. My fingers take a few minutes to uncurl, habituated as they are to the hafts of tools, and I spread open the Kodak newsletter to read while I wait, anchoring the corners with shears and the sweating thermos.

The company is turning a profit once again, always a good sign. I worked there as an engineer for thirty years. I discovered ways to make faster film—film that developed images with little light. Eugene was a banker, an investor, what they call in the papers now an entrepreneur. He made a lot of money. He was also an Olympic swimmer; twice, he set world records. He would get letters from other men offering to have sex. Nothing made him madder, but it meant he was noticed, somebody, a face, a name people remembered. I never once received a letter from a stranger and few enough from friends. Even at Kodak my work went unheralded.

I first realized we were headed for different futures at Yale. Both Skull and Bones, I was probably the least likely member ever and he one of the likeliest. I know why they let me in. A year after Eugene graduated he came back for a dance. Standing in a smoky back hallway, fumbling with my cuffs before entering the crowded room, I overheard Eugene talking with a few of the upper classmen, who told him they'd inducted me only because of him. He laughed, adjusting his tie, and said he wasn't surprised; he'd never thought me Skull and Bones material. I wondered even then if I wasn't meant to overhear them, and about what I should do. If the situation had been reversed, I knew Eugene would have resigned.

Eugene must have seen from my face that I'd heard. He was still adjusting his tie in the mirror, jutting his chin out to be sure the collar rested just so, and he said to his reflection words that were obviously intended for me. "Haven't you learned to lie yet?" It seemed a point of honor with him that he had.

I wasn't quite sure what he meant, but I took it to be comforting and let him lead me by the shoulder into the dance, and, though often burning with shame, stuck out three years in that club, an inch at a time.

Done with lunch, I fold up the wax paper for reuse, bag it, then push up off the tree. I see myself for a moment walking toward the rest of our family stones as if I were a stranger crossing the dirt roads and meadows: crickets buzzing, the sun beating down, a white shirt almost glowing in the light, dust rising to cover my shoes. Thousands have walked these paths before me. I can almost see their footsteps worn into the green grass. Early on Eugene found the care I took with graves morbid, a long attending on death. Nearer the end, studying stones, he seemed to think differently. He walked the cemetery's rutted roads with me, evidently recalling his own childhood memories, asked questions about our more distant relatives, stopped often at the empty plot beside Olivia's. He was ready, I think.

I liked those walks, and that he came to rely on me. I helped plan his estate, the sale of his house and the distribution of those possessions he worried his daughters would fight over, made the arrangements for his funeral. He seemed to want me near him in the end, and no one else.

Sandra came to see him twice, but he wouldn't let her in. Those last months, he allowed no one but me to see him without his dentures.

The stones are brilliant white in the afternoon sun, scrubbed weekly with bleach and water. The chlorine smell reminds me of summer mornings outside our kitchen, the maids on their knees scouring the floor with the sudsy water, ranks of purple impatiens spilling over the walk. Eugene would take his bicycle from the garage and leave without saying good-bye. I keep up all the family graves—cousins, aunts, uncles, parents, nephews. Most of our family's graves had fallen into disrepair when I started—it had been years since many had been cared for, decades for some. Toppled stones, chipped names and dates, stones grassed over completely. I started after Abigail's death, researching where many of the people were buried, digging through aunts' and uncles' attics for family letters. I asked Eugene if he had any. He hadn't.

There are Thomases and Wentworths and Wittons. I know about Gwyneth, who wanted to marry at thirteen, bowed to her parents objections, and married at fourteen. Twelve children later, aged twenty-six, she was dead. I had to buy her a new stone; the old one was illegible. Her parents built the largest mausoleum in the city. Nearby are other relatives' graves. One, Porter Witton, left town for sixty years, living as a tramp, and was returned only after death. He appeared one evening at an inn near Woldoboro, Maine, gave a gold pocket watch as security against his lodging expenses, then declined supper and went upstairs to bed. The next morning, when food was brought to him, he re-

fused it, saying that as he had no money he could not expect
to eat. Six days later he died, probably from starvation. The
innkeepers sold the watch and shipped him home. His sister, Mindwell, is buried nearby. She had a brief span of
glory, three weeks as skipper of her husband's ship. Two days
out of Rio he died of yellow fever, as did the first mate, and
she pickled his body in an unused beef barrel and took com-
mand of the ship, having learned navigation from her husband on their many voyages. His grave is at one remove
from hers, displaced by her second husband's.

This knowledge is not morbidity. If it weren't for me, no
one would keep up the graves. And each of them, in some
way, calls up memories. Now, when my knees are sore from
kneeling, or the sun climbs high enough to make the day too
hot, I sometimes pause in my rounds and try to remember
not only my own but what I imagine to have been Eugene's
memories as well.

It is a beautiful cool June Sunday and I am sitting in church.
The men smell of talc and cologne, the women of lavender
and roses. Sunlight streams through the stained glass windows, and looking up, I feel like I am inside a jeweled box.
A breeze blows through the open church doors, rattling the
thin pages of my hymnal.

Singing the hymns, the minister's high voice sends me
into reverie. Aside from the war I traveled only twice, once
to the Holy Land, once to Italy, taking both trips in the middle of winter so as to escape our dreadful weather. In Italy,
in a small walled town in the Perugian hills, I stumbled
across a museum dedicated to grasses. At first I thought I

was imagining things. Except for the Latin terminology I couldn't read the exhibits—I spoke no Italian—and the white-haired old woman in a black dress who took my money was either deaf or pretending to be, but I photographed each display case and the plaques saying what they held, then had the photographs enlarged and translated when I returned home.

The day was warm and sunny when I entered the museum. I came out to a violet dusk, the stone buildings blue, water glimmering in the gutters after a shower, iron gratings rumbling as they closed. There was a fresh chill wind. I couldn't believe my good fortune. I still have the pictures: a smoky vial of vernal-grass perfume, clear glass made from melted wheat straw, topaz-yellow glass made from barley, illustrations of how on all grasses the sheaths lap successively left and right, just as the leaves are borne alternately on opposite sides of the stem. Technically, this is called two-ranked growth. One of the plaques discoursed on grass's ubiquity and anonymity; many things we don't think of as grasses are—corn, wheat, oats, reeds, hay, mosslike grasses in cold countries, bamboo and sugarcane in hot. I don't know who had built the museum, or why, but really it didn't matter. Some kindred spirit, I supposed, interested in what much of the world found uninteresting. It is odd connections such as that on which I am counting.

I haven't spent any of the money Father and Mother left me. I thought of setting up a fund to ensure the upkeep of our graves, investing the principal and using the interest to pay a man to weed and trim the various graves a few times each year, but I am gambling on Sandra to take up where I will at some point leave off.

This is the way I've come to see it. Family is a loop you can't escape, and though at first I resisted that idea—almost resented it—I've come to find comfort in it: the constancy even of things that make you raw. After Eugene's funeral Sandra began asking questions. About him, about us, about our lives as children. She has Olivia's long-necked beauty. I remember the first stirrings of my own interest after a funeral in this same church years ago. The minister had just snuffed the altar candles and their smoke curled slowly toward the vaulted ceiling, where the echoes of the minister's voice and the mourners' song and the organ's bass notes still lingered like a presence, and I realized, seeing that transformation from flame to rising smoke, that the service imitated the soul's birth and passage and ascension. It was as if a single string had suddenly vibrated with sound deep inside my chest. I always feel that same note now at the end of a good service, during the few seconds where everything echoes—sights and sounds and memories—before people begin moving and talking, set loose again into the material world.

I had asked questions then, too. A few days ago, Sandra called again, asking if she could accompany me to visit the graves, so this morning I am not surprised to see her here, her tanned face demurely hidden beneath a straw hat, her white teeth showing when she sings. In my jacket, I feel the notebook's comforting solidity against my breast. This is not Sandra's church, nor do I know if she is especially reli-

gious or even religious at all. I am gambling that her interest is genuine. Not gambling, really; I have thought about it
for a long time. Yes, I tell myself here in the church, listening to the psalms—songs of captivity and return—Eugene
was my brother and Sandra is my great-niece and Eugene was
her grandfather, but those are just words and do little to un-
ravel the mystery. Like Adam, we have named the world but
not deciphered it.

About the Author

PAUL GRINER has a bachelor's degree in history and master's degrees in romance languages and literatures from Harvard and in creative writing from Syracuse University. He had a Fulbright Grant to Portugal, and has worked as a carpenter, painter, tour guide, and truck driver. His stories have appeared in *Story, The Graywolf Annual Four, Ploughshares, Bomb, Glimmer Train,* and *Playboy.* He lives with his family in Kentucky, where he is an assistant professor of English at the University of Louisville.

About the Type

This book was set in Perpetua, a typeface designed by the English artist Eric Gill, and cut by The Monotype Corporation between 1928 and 1930. Perpetua is a contemporary face of original design, without any direct historical antecedents. The shapes of the roman letters are derived from the techniques of stonecutting. The larger display sizes are extremely elegant and form a most distiguished series of inscriptional letters.